THE WOODS WITHIN

by Dr. Milo Yoder Jr.

To Rachel, a classmate
Enjoy! Milo

DORRANCE
PUBLISHING CO
EST. 1920
PITTSBURGH, PENNSYLVANIA 15238

9/25/2025

Dorrance Publishing Co
585 Alpha Drive
Suite 103
Pittsburgh, PA 15238
Visit our website at *www.dorrancebookstore.com*

ISBN: 978-1-6366-1236-2
eISBN: 978-1-6366-1823-4

This novel is dedicated to my wife, Judy
and to my son Erik Yoder and daughter Jennifer Johovich.

Preface

The author was inspired to write this novel by the interest gener-ated from the television documentary, *The Amish: Not to Be Mod-ern*, in which he was featured. The novel, *The Woods Within*, is a fictionalized memoir based on Yoder's intimate knowledge of the Amish way of life.

He grew up in an Amish family as the youngest of nine children, rebelled by going to high school, and by age twenty-one left the group to continue higher education. He maintained a psychoanalytic psycho-therapy practice in Chicago for fifty years and is currently retired.

While many of the events and experiences described in the novel are based on true stories, the characters in the book are products of the author's imagination and are composites of Amish people he once knew.

Prologue

"Frisky's dead. He is really gone," Jake repeated to himself over and over. He could not believe what he knew to be true. He stared at the endless toll road leading through the flat Indiana farmland. But what he saw was his dog, his soul mate of fifteen years, lying face-down in blood-spattered snow.

Driving home in the clear December air should have been easy. But it wasn't. Driving through his tears and memories made it difficult to watch the road. Memories of hunting together, playing tag, and tossing the green walnuts for Frisky to chase clouded the view of the road.

He was glad to be alone. Alone he felt safe. Safe enough to cry, even at the age of twenty-five. Alone in the car he watched himself with his dog as he listened to the soothing hum of tires on tar. He tried to forget the parting shot, but the scene kept coming back. Frisky's dead. But what hurt the most, what he couldn't believe, was how he died.

"I can't believe my father did it. Just can't believe it. It seems so long ago, so impossible, so far away. Just last month it happened."

Jake had gone home for Thanksgiving. His sister Sarah, her husband, and their five children had arrived the day before. They filled up the four bedrooms of the big white country house so he slept on a blanket on the living room floor close to the radiator.

It snowed in the morning. By the time the morning milking was finished the ground was blanketed with two inches of fluffy snow. He heard his father remark to his brother-in-law, "Good tracking snow. Just right for hunting, ya?" He had not heard him say that Frisky was getting too old to survive the winter.

After breakfast the three men readied their shot guns and started off toward the woods, for their traditional Thanksgiving rabbit hunt. Being experienced hunters, they walked in silence. Once inside the woods they spoke only with gestures.

They followed the creek whose north snow-covered bank was dotted with fresh squirrel, raccoon, fox, and rabbit tracks. The snow tracks told them all they needed to know, like road signs along the highway. The hunting was easy. They showed which animals were there, how long ago, which direction they headed, and the paths they were using for the water holes.

Within an hour they had their rabbits. The hunt ended. They left the woods still walking about twenty yards apart and entered the clearing on the east side. Jake saw Frisky romping in the field ahead. Frisky loved the hunt. He wanted more. His white fur looked dirty-gray against the fresh snow. A shot exploded. Jake jumped, frightened. From the corner of his eye he saw Frisky thud face down into the snow. Bits of blood and fur exploded into the air as he was going down. In horror and disbelief Jake turned to his right. Smoke rolled out of his father's gun.

Unthinking he yelled, "You shot my dog. My Frisky. Shot him. Killed my dog."

His father stared back looking puzzled, uncomprehending and finally replied, "I said he was getting too old for the winter."

. . .

In three short hours Jake would reach his childhood home that still belonged to another century, another culture, a place of horses and buggies and kerosene lamps. Alone, in his red Corvair he remembered the years of struggle growing up Amish, the years before he took a different road his father still traveled.

This is Jake's story.

Chapter One

The Weather Balloon

Jake was starving. At the sound of the bell he darted from his desk at the back of the classroom to the rear seat of the yellow school bus for the long ride home. He liked back seats. From there he could watch and think. He saw Katie enter and take a front seat. He couldn't tell if she smiled at him or he just imagined it. She was getting more and more shy. Lately she had trouble looking at him when they greeted. He wondered if her timidness had something to do with her body changing. She was beginning to look like a woman which her loose-fitting Amish dresses could not even disguise.

Jake watched the English kids on the bus yelling and chatting. They seemed so free, boisterous, and never seemed to run out of things to say. Finally, the bus reached the gravel roads and only Amish were left to be dropped off. Katie left with her four sisters and two brothers. As the bus pulled away they turned and waved goodbye, all except for Katie. Jake began to wonder about the meaning of this, but his stomach grabbed his attention instead.

He ran right from the yellow school bus straight for the tomato patch with Frisky yelping beside him. He was always starving right after

1

school and his dog, and soul mate, waited by the walnut tree beside the mailbox once he saw the bus with its cloud of dust approaching the Mast home. Yeah, he was starving. School lunches only seemed like a meager snack compared to the huge spread he was used to at home where the noon meal was their main meal of the day, the one they called dinner.

It was three-thirty in the afternoon, still very early for Jake. An Amish day usually did not end until all the farm chores were finished around eight in the evening. In only a few more months he would be fourteen years old and already he had the appetite and strength of more mature boys. His full name was Jacob Mast, but he liked to be called Jake. He liked his English name even though some of his Amish friends still called him by the Pennsylvania Dutch, Checky, Checky Masht, when they wanted to tease him.

Sometimes the teasing was more serious when they were worried that Jake was showing signs of wanting to be too English as shown by his interest in excelling in school. It seemed they needed to remind him who he was, where he belonged. He did not like being reminded.

The early tomatoes were a favorite after-school snack for Jake.

He was so hungry today he did not even bother to stop at the house for a salt shaker. He could only find four fairly ripe ones today. He gently pulled them off the stems by holding them with his left hand and snapping the stem by pinching it between the index finger and thumb of his right hand. He wiped off the tomato on his shirt tail, then took his time savoring each bite, being careful the squirt of each bite landed inside his mouth, not on his school clothes. After all, this was only Tuesday and this shirt, suspenders, and barndoor pants were his school outfit for the week. He was still hungry and began to scan the one-acre truck patch for the tomato row when he saw the afternoon sun darken from bright orange to an eerie red as it was blanketed by huge rolling thunder clouds. He guessed the storm was still five miles away as he stood in awe watching the Almighty paint the western horizon with furious strokes of orange and yellow, blood red, and flashing white lights enveloped in pitch black billows.

God was angry, very angry, perhaps? Or so his mother would say. He no longer believed this, he told himself, and yet he felt an inner body tension rising as if he did.

"I'm not taking a chance of finding out all by myself out here," Jake trembled and ran the hundred yards past the white barn to the house. He went into the house through the large family kitchen and tried to conceal his fear when he saw his mother preparing supper while she watched the brewing storm from the west windows. "Looks like a little rain I guess," Jake said as casually as he could.

"It looks more to me like God may be trying to tell us to mend our ways. The storm is black and angry. Look at that sun. It looks blood red. Now it's behind the black clouds. Jesus told us to be ready for his Second Coming. Oh! I hope we are all ready. Hell, everlasting fire! That's what's waiting for us if we're not."

"But Mom, we are good Amish."

"Are we now?" his mother blurted, full of fear and sarcasm. "You know I never wanted to move here. Why, some of these Amish own tractors, and now your father even wants to buy a bicycle. Look at your suspenders, store-bought! How Amish is that? Oh! God have mercy on us. I don't know what's to become of us. Listen to that wind, it's screaming." She fell on her knees and prayed. "O, Gott Vater im himmel...," and her voice trailed off as Jake ran out of the room.

He shook with fear inside but only a deep anger came out in a yell. "Oh, Mother you're getting beside yourself again," he said as he bounded up the stairs to his room. But what if she was right. Right that God is a vengeful God; a God quick to anger, swift to punish. He just could not believe God would care about the length of their hair, about whether or not they used bicycles, or had rubber tires on their wagon wheels.

A scream came from downstairs; not an angry scream, a scream of fear, of helplessness, of trepidation.

"Checky, komm hier," she yelled.

"I'm coming, Mother," Jake tried to calm her as he hurried down two steps at a time. She looked so helpless, white with fear. Tears were streaming down, her cheeks. Her plain brown apron was torn and her white organdy hair covering was hanging loosely from the tying strings around her neck, showing graying hair pulled straight back with a part in the middle.

Now in a timid, soft voice with her brown eyes locked on his she said, "Jake, I don't know where your father is. I hope he is right with God because I just looked out the window. I think, I think Jesus is coming. Right in the clouds. Like the Bible said he would." She took his hand. "Come, let's go on the north porch and wait for Him. We'll wait. Just wait for Him. I hope He will see us worthy to take us back to heaven with Him."

Jake began to cry as they walked arm in arm to the porch. The storm had strangely calmed. The wind fell still, deathly still. To the southwest the sky was black with streaks of swirling gray showing huge, powerful currents threatening the earth. To the northwest, high above the dark clouds, they saw Him. They saw Him in a small vertical shaft of white light. They stood in quiet awe and fear. Fear and foreboding, hoping against hope for mercy, mercy and forgiveness for their sins. They stood there, arm in arm. Tears streamed down their cheeks as they watched the white robes flowing in the white shaft. They waited and watched in fear. Time stopped. The End was here.

"Come on, Jake, time to milk the cows," Jake's father startled them.

"How can you think of such a thing now?" Mother accused. "Don't you see that Jesus is coming down in the clouds? Look up there. We should go warn the neighbors. Maybe there is still time to save them."

"Go ahead, I've got milking to do. You, too, Jake."

The spell was broken. Jake was relieved, yet very troubled. He had just seen all his known and unimaginable sins flash before him. He followed his father out to the barn but just to be safe, he climbed up into the hay loft to his secret place, knelt down and prayed for forgiveness for his sins, and for any sins he might have committed, even those he did not yet know about. He prayed and prayed, but still did not feel forgiven.

Neither did he find relief when an English neighbor stopped by to pick up a gallon of milk and asked whether they happened to see the new weather balloon.

"The what?" Jake blurted out.

"The new weather balloon. I heard on the radio that the weather bureau was experimenting with a balloon. What they're trying to find out I don't know, but I'm sure it won't change the weather any," he added with a chuckle.

"Guess not," Jake replied as he turned away hiding his embarrassment. He felt foolish and stupid.

Later, up in his room he still could not shake his feelings of having been made a fool of by his own emotions. He felt embarrassed, confused. His guilty feelings persisted and still felt just as real as the weather balloon itself. Yet, he knew his feelings were not coming from a real fear of something outside, but from something he believed. Nothing made sense and relief did not come. Gradually he felt himself getting more and more angry; it kept him from falling asleep for a long time.

Chapter Two

The Earth Is Flat

It was Saturday, already almost a week since Jake and his mother had stood there in fear and trembling. The feeling kept coming back with the memory of the weather balloon. His heart beat fast and his hands got sweaty. He had just come in from the hay field where he was cutting the second crop of the season. His father wasn't home from the mill yet, so Jake went to his private nook in the hay mow before starting the milking. He knew he had to start the chores soon because the family was invited to Bishop John's for dinner tonight.

All week he kept moving back and forth from two powerful feeling states, from scared to sarcastic anger. When he remembered the balloon he felt scared, even frightened, about the Judgement Day coming and he worried himself sick that he might sin just a second before Jesus burst from the clouds with not enough time to make a quick confession, knowing he would be banished to everlasting, burning fire in hell, forever and ever. He shuddered. "I would never see my father and mother again; or my brother or sister; forever exiled in hell, isolated, alone, burning in flames that never go out; with no rest or escape."

Fire was real, powerfully awesome and frightening, like a furious, wrathful God. He lingered in the hay mow and vividly recreated the memory of the fire that destroyed the Stauffer's barn that burned to the ground. He remembered running as fast as his ten-year-old legs could go as he trailed his father and brother Joe to the burning barn.

It happened on a late summer evening, right after supper. Jake joined his father on the porch to watch the storm. The sky to the north was dark, almost black, from the storm clouds that bunched up like millions of black cobras ready to strike with fiery jagged tongues of lightning. Together they saw the one white streak of lightning turn to yellow and then into a red ball as it struck the Stauffer's barn only a mile away. The barn exploded like a match. His father yelled upstairs to Joe, but by the time they reached the place on the run, the roof and massive beams had already collapsed into a heap, trapping the livestock and horses. There was nothing to do, but helplessly watch the inferno from a safe distance.

The next day Jake joined Joe and his father to help clean up, after the fire was spent. They came across burned carcasses of horses and cows. When Jake found a partially charred colt—its rump and rear legs had been burned almost to the bone, but its head and neck were twisted in a little pool of water—he nearly fainted. He vaguely recalled running into their apple orchard where he threw up. He had stayed there for a long time until he heard his father calling for him.

"Where were you? I was looking all over for you." His father sounded angry.

"Oh, I was just in the orchard. I had to go relieve myself," Jake tried to sound matter-of-fact. The last thing he wanted was to hear his father's and brother's ridicule for being scared and having the stomach of a girl. Never could he let them know how scared he was of going to hell and that seeing the burned colt made him think of burning in hell.

But he did ask, "Dad, do you think the horses suffered a long time before they died? Do they feel the flames burn their flesh?"

"What difference does it make? They're dead. We have work to do. Grab that end and we'll move this beam out of the way."

Jake lifted his end and asked, "Do you think they die from the smoke?"

"Ya, the vet said they usually die from breathing the smoke," his father replied curtly. Jake stopped asking any more questions when he heard a familiar exasperated mutter, "You and your questions!"

Jake felt confused and wondered why his father did not seem to share his fear and dread of hellfire and damnation. Maybe he did and he just did not talk about it. Perhaps he just worked instead. The other week, when the weather balloon scared them, his father had also merely said, "We have work to do." After all, it was not Jesus coming in the clouds to send us all to hell. It was a mere weather balloon. How can feelings be so strong and yet so wrong? Just then he heard the center barn doors screech on the steel track as his father pushed them open.

"Check, wo bist du?"

"I'm up in the mow. Just throwing the hay down for the milkers," Jake yelled back as he grabbed the three-pronged hay fork.

Jake swept out the cow stanchions, cleaned the gutter, and sprinkled fresh lime on the cement floor in preparation for milking. He was glad his father was in a good mood. He was humming while he unloaded the cow feed he brought back from the mill.

Jake opened the west door and the cows led by Bossy rushed in like unruly children to their assigned places.

"Isn't it something how the cows know their places?"

"Of course, they know their places. We certainly spent enough time teaching them where to go," his father replied.

"No, no. I meant their places with each other. Bossy clearly is the boss. Betsy comes next. She bosses all the others except Bossy. Lilly is the third-level boss. Actually, I've been watching them and I think I've figured out the first five-level bosses, but I still can't place the last six."

"Why is that important? All I care about is that they know where to stand for milking," his father said with a tone more of puzzlement than criticism.

They finished the milking. They had worked side by side, mostly in a pleasant silence, except for his father's brief comments about how empty it seemed around there without the others. Jake had felt hurt by this because he knew his father missed not having Joe and Sarah around because they did not seem to have their "heads in the clouds," as his father liked to put it. Jake ignored the implication. He wanted his father in a good mood when they went out to visit the bishop's house tonight.

"Hurry up Jake. I promised John's Ida we would get there before the sun went down," his mother cheerily yelled into the bathroom.

"Be right there." Even though they had moved into this farmhouse more than a year ago, Jake still could not believe the house had an indoor bathroom with running water, a sink, and a flushing toilet. He was glad this house was originally made for an English family, otherwise they would have had to use the outhouse even in the winter, just like on the old place. This house even retained electrical sockets with push-button switches. Of course, the electricity was disconnected when the previous Amish family had lived there. Fortunately, Jake thought, this Amish group did not ask them to get rid of the bathrooms, since the bathrooms were built into the original structure.

"Your father's gone out already to hitch up."

"Coming, right away." Jake picked up the kerosene lamp and held it close to the mirror to have one quick look at his hair. He wanted to look good for Susy, the bishop's fourteen-year-old daughter. He had overheard gossip that she sometimes got a little loose if you could get her to play in the hay mow. This was hard to believe since she always seemed so proper and even a little shy. "Oh, well, might as well be prepared," he thought as he went down the stairs.

Jake's mother and father were waiting for him in the topless buggy and Nellie was already prancing, eager to start off. Jake was pleased they were taking this buggy because he could sit by himself with his feet dangling from the truck bed, with his back toward the front. Besides, at his age he had become uncomfortable having to sit on anyone's lap. These single buggies only had one seat made for two people.

"Watch out for the spokes."

"Mother, how old do you think I am?" Jake yelled over his shoulder.

"I guess I keep forgetting. But you know what happened to your cousin Joey."

"He was just six years old, not thirteen." Jake had heard that story so many times he was sick of it. Joey's older brother was sitting in the back holding his foot at just the right angle to the wheel so that the spokes of the wheel made a dull rat-ta-tat sound on the heel of his shoe. Joey also tried this but the wheel caught his foot and broke his leg in two places. They raced the horse and buggy to the nearest doctor, about an hour away. They screamed the whole way there.

Jake tuned out his parent's conversation. He was glad Nellie picked up her speed as she paced along the blacktop. They turned east. This gave him a full view of the sunset. Far into the distant horizon filmy clouds looked like huge floating bands of organdy see-through cloth that caught the fading rays, weaving them into shades of purples, pinks, oranges, and reds. The grandeur left him speechless. He wondered how a God who could create such a picture could also be a harsh judge that bursts through the same sky to catch you by surprise.

"Whoa, Nellie, whoa." They turned into the long dirt lane. It led to the white frame house with the blue trim around the windows. Bishop John was sitting on the porch rocker waiting for their arrival. He came out as Nellie walked to a stop.

"Vie geht's, Amos?"

"Gut. Und wie bist du, Chohn?" his father returned the friendly greeting.

"Here, Mary, let me help you down."

Jake and his mother were particularly fond of Bishop John. Sometimes he suspected his mother liked him because she felt safer from eternal damnation if the bishop was friendly to her. But it was true that John Bontrager was a soft-spoken, mild mannered, gentle person who genuinely seemed to like people. Jake did not like it when it was the bishop's turn to preach because of his long-winded, sing-song style, but he fondly admired him for his warmth and caring. He was a rather handsome man, about fifty-five, with strong shoulders, graying hair that almost covered his ears, and a long gray beard that he kept neatly brushed. Jake looked up to him as a wise old gentleman who was sincerely devout and humble.

"Hello, come on in. Supper's almost ready. Susy just has to finish the cherry pie," Ida Bontrager bubbled excitedly as she came out to the porch wiping her hands on her white apron. "I see the men coming in from the stable. Jake, you are sure getting bigger every time I see you. Why don't you go on in and visit with Susy while she finishes the pie? She wouldn't mind."

"No thanks, that's alright. I'll just wait for the men to join us." Jake was surprised how shy he felt and wished he had not heard that little gossip about Susy. Maybe it was not even true, he thought.

Everyone was going in from the porch when Susy came out of the kitchen. She shyly nodded a greeting and whispered to her mother that the food was ready. She and Jake avoided looking at each other directly and he assumed she was just as relieved as he was that the seating arrangement did not have them facing each other.

"Hum." John cleared his throat and immediately there was silence and all eyes were on him. Jake knew this was the signal for saying grace before the meal. The bishop began his prayer in High German, then switched to Pennsylvania Dutch as he added more personal extemporaneous comments, even mentioning Jake in his prayer. Jake was very surprised by this personal touch and felt even more shy. At the amen his mother was looking at him with a huge smile, as if she had just been supremely honored. This both pleased and irritated him.

"Now just help yourself. We'll pass the food clockwise." Ida said, clearly the one in charge once her husband had said grace. For once Jake was glad that it was usually the custom for the adults to talk and for the younger ones to eat and keep quiet unless spoken to. He was very hungry. The roast beef was cooked very well-done and served with gravy and mashed potatoes. Dishes of carrots, peas, and green beans were also passed around along with loaves of warm home-made bread and strawberry jam. He ate to his heart's content and was only vaguely aware of the men talking about how their crops were doing this year. After several more rounds of meat and potatoes, Susy left the table to serve the cherry pie.

"Susy will serve her pie and we'll see how good it came out. Right Jake?" Ida asked.

"I'm sure it is very good," replied Jake.

"For those who might not like fruit pie, we also made pecan and custard pies. So help yourself," Ida proudly announced.

She had long been known for her excellent baking skills, and Jake wondered if Susy felt hurt by this. He couldn't tell. He couldn't see her face since she had walked back into the kitchen. Cherry pie was his favorite and this one was very good with the crust just the right flaky consistency.

Jake caught Susy's eye and said quietly, "Your pie is very good. One of the best I've had."

"Thank you," she responded as she blushed and looked down on her plate.

"Well, what do you think, Amos? Have you had enough?"

"That was very good. Thank you for having us over for dinner, John."

"You are welcome. Why don't we go out for a little walk and let the women take care of the dishes. Jake, why don't you come with us?"

When they got outside Jake's father said he had to go to the barn for a spell so John and Jake stood on the south lawn and waited. Jake felt he should make a little conversation. "Isn't that sky beautiful? It is so lit up by all the stars."

"Ya, it is God's wonderful handiwork. It's a good thing, too, that nobody around here has electricity. It is so dark out here in the country it makes the stars shine more brightly. Ya, God made a beautiful universe."

"Isn't it amazing though, how everything works together so well? I mean, here we are on this round spinning ball, held on by gravity, and just a small part of a whole universe, maybe even many, many universes."

"What do you mean by that kind of talk?"

Alerted, Jake had never heard Bishop John's voice so loud and angry.

"Don't you know that the earth is flat? The Bible talks about the four corners of the earth," his anger was turning into a scolding. "It sounds to me like you have been paying too much attention to that worldly wisdom, that science stuff. Young man, you better listen a little better in church."

"I, I guess so," Jake stammered, averting his eyes. He was crushed, hurt, and deeply disappointed. His stomach seemed to collapse onto the heavy meal. He had only been trying to make a little conversation. His heart sank. His fondness, his admiration for the bishop seemed to be melting into thin air.

"How can he say that? How can he believe such a thing? The earth is flat!" he thought.

"Sorry you had to wait so long," Jake finally heard his father interrupt the silence.

"That's okay, Amos, I was having a talk here with Jake. I think you better talk to him about some of that science stuff he is learning in school," Jake heard the bishop saying as he and his father started walking.

"Hey Jake, aren't you coming with us?" his father called back when he realized only two of them were walking.

"No, that's okay. I have to go do something," Jake said as he headed for the barn. "Gee, he probably also believes in Jesus weather balloons," he thought. He felt himself getting more and more angry.

Chapter Three

Heat of the Day, July, 1955

It was five A.M., and the July sun's rays signaled the stealthy night creatures to go into hiding while stirring up the farm animals for another day. The discordant symphony of rooster crows, baas, oinks, whinnies, and moos certainly awakened the Amish farmer if the sun's light and early heat had not already done so. But this Sunday morning Jake hadn't stirred, even to his mother's calls. "Jake, it's time to get up," his mother yelled up for the third time.

"Coming, I'm coming," he growled sleepily while dropping his farm shoe on the hardwood floor hoping she would take that to mean he was already getting dressed. "I've got to get up, Dad will milk more than his share," he thought, as he drifted back into the naked arms of his morning dream girl who had mysteriously appeared ever since he had turned thirteen. For a whole year now this dream would often visit him in the mornings. Her name was Katie. A classmate. His secret love who could only manage a blushing "hi" at school even though her full breasts and shapely legs were hidden by the full-skirted, black, ankle-length dress with a high neckline. But in the morning, Katie would come to him, shamelessly undress, lie down on the bed beside him, and beckon him to enjoy her body's silky secrets. This morning, once again, she came to his bedroom, and with an almost casual air, unpinned her black flowing dress, slowly, deliberately let it slide from her shoulders, over her bare breasts, and then—her eyes, clear brown eyes that never left his, showed not a hint, not a trace of shame, of guilt as they beckoned him. She lay down on the bed beside him, but not too close, so he could still feel the power, the force of her eyes that strangely held no reproach. He kept his shady untrusting eyes riveted on hers, then slowly, carefully moved his hand toward her white, silky smooth thigh and still her eyes said yes. He reached to touch her left breast when—

"Get up this minute," came the scream as his mother started up the stairs.

Katie vanished with the scream, but the sinful erection remained as Jake had only enough time to kneel beside the bed in mock prayer. His mother's thundering foot-stomps reached the doorway, and her yell was cut in half; the last half hung in the still, tense air as he heard the door quietly latch and her footsteps fade away. His trick had worked before, but whether it was because he was praying or because he was dressed only in briefs, he never knew for sure.

Jake tore into his clothes, rolled his suspenders into his fist, and slammed them against the closet wall. "Damn these stupid clothes. Damn this early getting up shit. Christ sake, it's 1955." He retrieved his suspenders, buttoned them to his barndoor pants, and controlled his impulse to smash the kerosene lamp. "We could at least get electricity," he fumed under his breath as he bounded down the stairs. He rushed out through the north porch to avoid Mother's "you're going to hell" look, slammed the door, and ran to the cow barn where his father was already sweating from the July heat. His father didn't say a word; just kept on milking, his blatant anger rushing through his muscular arms and hands as they rhythmically squeezed the teats. "That's right, you silent son of a bitch," Jake thought as he picked up a pail and three-legged stool, "just let me hang myself by my own guilt. Christian love, my ass. How come it feels like hate?"

"Jake," his father began as if no bad feelings had filled the silence, "I promised Joe Schrock we would help him unhitch the horses this morning since church services will be held there today."

"Yes, I remember," Jake replied, relieved by the broken silence. His arm muscles settled into a relaxed rhythmical motion and the one-two, one-two beat of the milk squirts even seemed to relax Bossy as she resumed munching her hay. She was his favorite cow. She was steady and low-key, yet was sensitive to his moods. Once, twice she shifted in her stanchion, looked back at him with her big brown sympathetic eyes.

"Now, now Bossy," Jake soothed back. "Dad, did you milk the Kicker yet?"

"Not yet, but I thought I would have to do her next."

Jake heard a slight sarcastic edge in his father's tone and a shot of guilt ripped into his temple, once more sparking his rage. Trapped again! Between his guilt and his anger. Between his wish to be forgiven and his father's rebuff.

Bossy caught his tension through the teats. The one-two squirt beat changed to a double-time tempo as Jake raced to finish Bossy before his father finished Molly. But there was no way for Bossy to know why this race was survival itself. He could let the bastard milk the Kicker as payment for his rebuff, but he knew all too well from experience the price for this would be a church full of reproachful eyes. All day long!

They finished a tie, but Jake got to the ten-gallon can first, poured the milk into the strainer, and grabbed the chain hobbler off the hook.

"Whoa, now Betz. Take it easy," Jake tried to soothe the Kicker, but his voice gave his tenseness away. As he leaned down to hook the one end of the hobbler to the left rear leg, Betz kicked with the right rear. "Stop that!" Jake yelled as he dodged her long powerful legs. His stomach felt weak. If her near miss had hit the target his kneecap could have been shattered. "Now stop that! Cut it out!" he heard himself still yelling.

"Now why don't you stop it?" his father sounded contemptuous. "If a cow scares you, let me hobble her."

Jake stood up straight, his eyes fixed, his muscles rigid, bulging. And now the anger from the insult of insults easily overshadowed his fear. His father stood watching, saying nothing.

Slowly, deliberately, Jake walked right up to Betz, shoved her rear end against the wall, pinning her there, and in one quick, smooth motion, held both her rear legs with his right arm, clamped the hooks with his left hand, and tightened the chain until her rear legs couldn't move at all.

"That's no way to treat a cow," Jake heard his father mumble to himself as he walked away.

"Well, I guess we learn from example," Jake spit back one of his father's phrases. This struck hard and low. Not a word passed between them. Even when they had to move a 150 pound cattle trough together, their eyes never met. They finished the chores in silence and went in for breakfast.

Throughout the stilted silence they each removed their boots and set them on the grass outside the south porch to keep the manure stench from the immaculately clean house. Jake's mother tried to infuse a cheeriness into the painful silence the moment they entered the huge family kitchen that until recently had seated the five of them. Jake felt the sadness and the emptiness of the big house now that only three of them were left at home.

"Wash up Jake, breakfast is ready. You can start with the coffee soup. The eggs will be ready in a minute." Jake's mother's stream of chatter began to lighten his mood even though he knew the words were not meant to communicate anything except a tone of forgiveness, and to break the angry silence.

For this he loved her.

"Well, let's eat." Now even his father's voice signaled a conciliatory mood. Their heads bowed in prayer. "Herr, Gott, Water..." his father began and Jake trailed off to Katie's loving eyes, interrupted by the amen. He was startled finding his mother looking at him, as if she could read his thoughts, but then she smiled. His shoulders relaxed and Jake assumed it must have looked like he had been praying, simultaneously terribly relieved and sad that the truth had once again escaped discovery.

"As I mentioned in the barn," his father began. His eyes briefly met Jake's indicating a more friendly connection. "You and I have to help Joe Schrock with the horses. People will be arriving for church services about eight o'clock; especially the older folks who need help with unhitching, parking their buggies, watering, feeding, and tying up the horses."

"Yes, I know," Jake replied, his voice deliberately pleasant. He wished to give no sign of hostility about his father's compulsive habit of listing in detail all the steps involved. But behind the compliant look his thoughts raced rebelliously. "For God's sake, I already knew all the steps by age four. You think I'm dumb?"

Jake excused himself from the table and rushed to get dressed as quickly as possible so that he could avoid walking with his parents to the Schrock farm a mere half-mile away. He had already bathed the night before standing in a galvanized five-gallon tub that was set in the kitchen for Saturday night baths. Getting dressed for the bi-monthly Sunday services was very simple. He only owned one white shirt, a pair of dress socks, one pair of black-tie shoes, and one dark gray suit that years later in the American culture could have passed for a Nehru coat.

"I'm leaving now," Jake called out as he dashed out the back door to avoid any suggestions about walking together. Almost immediately he slowed his pace. It was already getting hot and a glance at the sun's position showed it was still only around seven-thirty. "Someday," he thought, "I'll buy me a pocket watch, or perhaps even one of those fancy watches the English boys wear on their wrists." He ambled across the twenty-acre clover hay field, barren from the recent second cutting. The stubbles scuffed up his polished shoes as he walked through the field and watched the red-wing black birds scattering a flock of cowbirds. The clipped field revealed a teeming life of darting field mice, scurrying rabbits, and the ever-present gophers. Suddenly, Jake sensed a presence. He halted to complete stillness, controlled his breathing; total instinctual awareness, no thinking, totally alert, but unmoving. Just as he began to think his intuitive sense was mere imagination his eye caught a slight movement to his left. There it was again, about eight feet away. He slowly edged closer, his heart pounding, muscles taut, fear rising. There was the blue racer, a six-foot snake eating a garter snake still hanging half-way out.

The stone-crunching sound of steel-rimmed buggy wheels on the gravel road brought Jake up short. He felt caught between his wish and his need. He gave in to the need to go to church. He ran, climbed the Schrock fence, jumped over the poison ivy, and arrived just in time to help with the horses.

During the next thirty minutes Jake was too busy to rest his thoughts on the blue racer or his morning dream; nevertheless, he was fully aware of Katie's arrival with her parents in their new double buggy, a two-seated carriage for families. He noted that the backless benches were arranged for service in the Schrock's new buggy shed instead of the house.

By nine o'clock sharp, the Foresinger announced the song number in a loud voice, startling Jake from an already encroaching reverie. The song leader, who remained sitting, began the chant-like melody in his gruff baritone. He sang the first word which lasted approximately a measure, then everyone joined. This procedure was repeated for each noteless line of *The Ausbund*, the Amish Hymnal, and everyone sang the melody in unison since harmony was forbidden. This bound of unity enhanced the mandatory sameness of hair-styles, dress, the make of the buggies, including even a horse's harness. However, for Jake the sound and look of unity was the screen that highlighted individualistic differences. Sometimes he could even feel like he almost belonged.

The beginning of the second verse signaled Bishop John to lead the ministers and deacons single file out through the wide center aisle for

20

their customary pre-service council meeting. All four wore their hair long. The rule was that the hair in the back had to reach down to the shirt collar and at least halfway over the ears. In front the hair was combed straight down and at approximately one-half inch from the eyebrows. Men were not allowed to part their hair, trim their beards, or wear a mustache.

Jake was keenly aware of the ministers walking slowly down the aisle as he carefully avoided eye contact with Bishop John by pretending to concentrate on the song. To Jake, these men in all their sameness appeared uniquely different, not only as personalities, but even in the variations of the hair style, color, texture, thickness, and length. The bishop had a long gray beard that thinned out to a point reaching almost to his navel. He was balding on top and the hair on the sides and back curled up to the indentation line made by his hat.

Jake watched the men file into the house. The deacon gently shooed the family dog away as he closed the door behind him. The second song was announced, the "Lob Lied," the praise song all Amish congregations sing at every service. Jake noticed some of the children were already getting restless and was glad his feet reached the floor. As a child he had dreaded the pain of sitting on a backless bench for three hours with only one break. He noticed the Schrocks had placed one of their house clocks in the shed for the service. Two and a half hours to go! "Now if we're lucky," Jake thought, "Bishop John will preach the 'anfang,' the beginning sermon, and Sam Miller will preach the main sermon." Sam Miller was a dynamic preacher who also tended to stop on time, while the bishop kept on and on in his sing-song tone until you felt like screaming.

The ministers filed back in from their meeting just as the last song ended, and unfortunately, Sam Miller was the first to preach. He stood in the aisle at the south, closed end of the shed and made the usual humility remarks that always irritated Jake.

"Dear Brothers and Sisters in the Lord," Sam began in a slightly sing-song rhythm. "I humbly beseech you to be patient with me today as I bring you the Word of God. There are others here who could do much better than I, but with God's help I'll do the best I can."

Jake wondered if no one else sensed the irony of such humble words coming from the most arrogant man present. He took flight from his irritation by drifting off to his morning dream, but then became aware the Katie of the dream was sitting somewhere across the room. He scanned the women's section noting the sameness of the organdy white material worn over the solid color dresses, colors ranging from shades of blue, green, pale yellow, and… There she was, across the aisle, two rows back, to the right. She wore a deep burgundy dress, the color easily showing through the synthetic organdy. The burgundy accented her natural rosy complexion and Jake quickly looked down and sank into a trance-like reverie of his dream, feeling the beginning of an erection.

"You will burn in hell, forever and ever," Sam's bellow broke through Jake's shield, "if you young people keep your sinful ways." Preacher Sam had steamed up to his hellfire sermon, filled with inuendo about the evils of sex. He was particularly effective since as a young man he had been known as the wildest during his sowing wild oats period. Of course, he never referred to sex directly, this was only implied, since the Amish learn from an early age that one is supposed to act as if sex doesn't exist, which pumps the impulse up to a fever pitch. Some of the mothers were beginning to cry; the men looked down; even the boys were deathly still. The guilt attacks kept coming at Jake like a swarm of angry hornets and he knew the only sensible thing to do was to hold very, very still, like the quarry being hunted for the kill.

"Be very still, be still," Jake was saying to himself, and then he sensed a movement. There it was again, to his left. He glanced up. There it was. The Schrock's family dog—acting funny. "Oh, no," he realized she was in heat. She was not merely being playful or even paying attention to the people a mere twenty feet away. At that moment another dog answered her call, sniffed and licked her rear, and proceeded to copulate in front of the whole congregation.

Preacher Sam kept going at full steam. The women were crying. The men still looked down. Jake was incredulous. Surely, they must sense, must see, must know what's happening. Then the young boys and girls started giggling and Jake saw the irony, and could hardly control his laughter. The whole shed seemed to vibrate with electricity as a quick glance showed that even some of the men couldn't pretend anymore. Finally, when it appeared the dogs had gotten stuck one of the men chased them away from view.

The comic relief temporarily scattered Jake's guilt attacks. For reasons he couldn't understand he felt a sense of relief, almost calm. Yet this all seemed strange, almost like night creatures who got confused and came out in the light of day. "I wonder," he mused, "Maybe there are others like myself who can't seem to keep the night and day stuff apart. Surely, a good Amishman must do that. Wonder if Joe was ever troubled like this."

His thoughts went to Sarah. She always seemed to know where she was going. She did as she was told, followed the rules, quit school at sixteen, met a nice Amish boy, was baptized as a formal member of the church, got married, and then had children. He wished he could be more like his sister, but knew that was hopeless for him.

Chapter Four

The Wrestling Match

Jake kept wrestling with his night shadows. He decided the answer must lie in making his commitment to the church. It worked for Sarah. It must work for him too. At the early age of fifteen he was formally accepted through the rite of instruction and baptism. His peers found this strange as their custom was to join just prior to getting married, about eighteen to twenty-one years of age. Instead of finding inner peace, he felt more and more confused.

He joined the formal instructional class with two others, Otis Miller who was twenty, and Rebecca Smucker, a sad teary-eyed girl of nineteen. On church-service Sundays, during the first congregational song, the three of them followed the line of ministers to their separate meeting place for religious instruction. Jake felt appalled with the meetings. The ministers assigned no readings of the Bible. They mainly briefed the class on the many rules of dress, hair length, and appropriate behavior toward the authority of the church leaders.

Unlike Otis and Rebecca, Jake studied the few Bible verses Bishop John used to support his instructions. On the second Sunday of confirmation Jake timidly asked the older Otis, "Do the German Scriptures John uses make sense to you?"

"Nah," he replied his face showing surprise to the question. "Just do as they say and you'll be fine. I never learned the High German anyway."

Jake did not tell Otis that since their last meeting he studied the verses in both German and English, using the English Bible his brother had left behind, hidden in his room. Otis's response clearly told Jake he was taking everything too seriously, too personally. Later he learned that Otis was joining church because he was soon getting married.

Rebecca never spoke. Much of the time she sat with her eyes cast down. Periodically she sniffled and wiped her tears. She always carried a white handkerchief initialed with an *R*. She followed all the dress codes to the letter. She wore a dark blue dress, black hose and lace shoes, a white organdy apron, and matching top that was meant to disguise her breasts. Her uncut hair, parted in the middle, was severely pulled back and roiled into a bun held up with hair pins. Her hair covering was a small white organdy cap held on by strings tied under her chin.

On the way to the last instructional Jake whispered to Otis, "That girl sure cries a lot."

Otis quietly replied, "Ya. Guess she feels bad about having to get married."

"Oh. I didn't know," Jake casually responded. But inside Jake felt a shock for he had not known Rebecca was pregnant.

Otis added, "From what I hear the fellow that got her in a bad way might not even be Amish."

During this last meeting Jake felt very tense. The information about Rebecca just added to his already churning stomach. He still felt confused. He read and reread the Bible; the part that says if he confessed his sins and believed in Jesus Christ he would be saved and forgiven. Still, Jake felt miserable, unforgiven.

At the end of the session Bishop John for the first time asked if there were any questions. In the thunderous silence that followed, Jake gathered his courage despite his trembling stomach and asked his burning question.

His voice shook when he asked, "I know that the Bible says if I confess my sins and believe in Jesus Christ, that he died for me, that I am then forgiven and saved. Why is it then, that I still feel so bad, so unforgiven, so guilty?"

A deathly silence filled the small room. Otis stared at Jake, astonished. Rebecca began to cry. The three ministers first looked stunned, looked down at their shoes, then almost as one turned toward Bishop John who was staring at his closed Bible on his lap and stroking his long beard.

Finally, the bishop responded without looking at Jake. "We Amish don't believe we can be 'saved.'" All we can do is be good Amish, follow the rules of the elders, and hope. All we can do is hope that in the end, at the Judgement Day, that God will have mercy and take us to heaven. If there are no more questions we will go ahead with the baptismal service in two weeks."

Jake was stunned. The bishop did not know, did not understand. Jake felt more alone than before. He would have to keep struggling by himself. He hoped the baptism held the answer. Maybe then he would feel better, feel forgiven. The baptismal service came and went. No magic happened. No answer came. He still felt rotten, guilty. All he knew was that even the bishop had no answer.

Jake gradually accepted the realization that he would have to live alone with his own personal struggles. Months passed. He had just turned sixteen and had grown to be quite muscular during this last year. While he was proud of his strength and his physique he had learned, of course as all Amish boys are taught, to keep his pride to himself and to portray a humble, almost obsequious demeanor. This value of at least appearing humble was not taught so much by verbal pronouncements as by the nonverbal disapproval of the adults. At the same time Jake readily sensed the pride his parents and friends felt about his ability to work like a horse and to keep up his end of a wrestling match.

"Why can I be proud of being strong and muscular, but have to act as if I'm not?" he kept puzzling to himself as the minister droned on in his sing-song sermon.

The church service was being held today in Levi Miler's barn in the large section between the hay mows with the steal track at the peak of the barn serving as a roost for several pigeons who cooed throughout the meeting. "They seem to have their own little amen corner," Jake amused himself while he also made sure none of the pigeons were directly overhead so he could ride with his imagination during this three-hour service instead of worrying when he would be hit by a dropping.

Riding his vivid imagination while sitting on the hard backless benches had become both his joy and his survival technique. It was also his time to puzzle about the inconsistencies that confronted him. The hidden message was that he could feel proud of himself, but only if he never communicated this in words. He had to at least talk humble at all times. Bragging was considered to be a serious sin. Yet he would be viewed as a sissy, if during a wrestling match, he did not show his strength and stamina. "This makes no sense," he mused. "Pride is pride, whether or not it is open or hidden."

His left eye caught a movement on the bench behind him. He saw there were some visitors today, four young men who looked like they were about seventeen or eighteen years old. One of them had removed his coat because of the heat and was rolling up his shirt sleeves revealing a hairy, muscular arm. He looked Jake in the eye, nodded imperceptibly, and put two fingers on his biceps. Jake immediately understood the whole proposition and returned one curt nod. The deal was set. This visitor had heard of Jake, wanted a wrestling match at two o'clock. For a moment he wished his reputation as a wrestler had not preceded the match. He much preferred the advantage that came with the unknown.

"And if God willing, we will meet for services in two weeks at the Hostetler place," Bishop Bontrager finally concluded his sermon.

"Why do they always feel so hopeless? Anyway, if some tragedy did interfere with the plans, they still would say it was God's will," Jake critically mused. For reasons he did not understand, this kind of circular thinking always got under his skin.

He felt his irritation moving into his biceps and forearms and during the final song, he began his preparation for the upcoming match by imagining from the challenger's physique what his weakness might be. He felt at a disadvantage since he did not know anything about the other guy except he seemed to emanate a kind of menace; a kind of sinister air, perhaps a meanness. Jake could not put his finger on exactly what he sensed about him, but intuited an animal quality. No, that was not quite it either. Finally the service was over and he filed out with the others and as he stepped into the sunlight, he heard from close behind him, "Hi, I'm Jim Cassidy."

Jake was startled. The guy spoke English. He didn't even have a Pennsylvania Dutch accent. His was not an Amish name; besides he had not noticed any non-Amish at the service. Jake kept his startled reaction deep inside and casually turned around to greet the stranger, this English who had long black hair cut in the Amish style and wore the homemade Amish suit; the one who had challenged him to a match.

"Hello, did you say your name was Chim?" Jake calmly asked in his own accented English while trying to appear friendly and unrattled.

"That's right, Jim Cassidy. And I hear you're supposed to be the hotshot tough guy in this district. Well, no one got the best of me where I come from and I would bet I could rip your butt."

Deep inside Jake recoiled from this direct, challenging, bragging tone of the rude outsider. He looked Amish but certainly knew nothing about being Amish. Jake looked down wanting Jim to think he was intimidated and merely asked, "And where is it that you come from?"

"Detroit," he replied loudly to the whole group of teens who had gathered around the two. Jake now knew that this Cassidy had been set up by one or more of the other Amish fellows who were hoping he would demolish Jim in the seemingly friendly atmosphere of an Amish wrestling match.

"Zeit fa essa," Erv interrupted as he walked up to Jake. The rest of the boys followed suit and went to the table for the noon meal of homemade peanut butter, molasses, bread, and pickles and beets. Jim had joined his buddies at the other end of the long table that was made by stacking several of the twelve-foot backless benches onto slotted wooden horses for this purpose. The table setters had not bothered to include benches for the teens to sit on, letting them eat standing up.

Jake was relieved that Jim was at the far end so he and Erv, his friend since early childhood, could discuss this rude stranger.

"Was vashe du?" Jake whispered.

"Nichts viele. Actually, I hardly know anything about him," Erv replied, "but I am sure that his so-called buddies are actually a bit embarrassed with him. I can't imagine why he wanted to join the Amish or why the other district is even considering letting him join. My father said he had only heard of such a thing once, an outsider joining the Amish! The idea! I don't care how he looks, he still could never be a real Amishman; look how he talks proud and acts rude. Anyway, he can only talk English."

"Surely the other district can't really accept him. He could just be dressing Amish for some other reason. Do you think?"

"I don't really know what to think, but I can tell you one thing, if he is as strong and tough as he talked, you are going to have your hands full this afternoon."

"Ya, I know what you mean," Jake said while he was debating whether to tell Erv about his sixth sense that there was something mean and sinister about this Jim. Instead, he said, "Come on Erv, I have to go take a leak and I'm sure all the women are away from the barn by now." So they walked to the horse stable where the men relieved themselves after the noon meal. But for some unknown reason Jake still could not bring himself to say anything about his suspicions about this

Cassidy fellow. Besides, there were other times Erv had made fun of Jake's ability to sense things about people that lay beneath the surface, so he decided to keep his thoughts to himself.

"How would you size him up?" Jake asked.

"By his mouth I would say you don't have a chance."

"Erv, you know what I mean," Jake was getting a little exasperated and nervous.

"What's the matter with you, Jake? You seem more nervous than usual before a match. I'll never forget when you threw that big English six-footer on his back and he didn't get up for five minutes. This Jim character is only about five feet eight I would guess. He is quite muscular, but your quickness is what wins the matches anyway. So, he is my height and I'd guess he weighs about the same and I haven't been able to best you for two years. I just don't see why you should have any real problem."

"Well, I just don't have a good feeling about it," Jake quietly replied.

"What is this, that sensing, feeling stuff again?" Erv saw that Jake was very serious. He had often noticed that whenever he became serious or very angry his voice would become lower, quieter and controlled. "I'll tell you what, before the match, get Joe to help me step in if Jim doesn't stick with our rules."

"Thanks. Where is a good place for it? I don't want to have the match on the lawn, a crowd would be there in no time and Mom would be furious if I stained my suit pants. Besides, Ellie has already seen me wrestle and she was not impressed like the other girls."

"Jake, you sure are taken with that girl. Is it her knockers or her brain? I can never figure it out. You're a bit weird, so I suppose you like the rarity of a brainy Amish girl."

"Get off it, Erv. I don't feel like being teased right now."

"Chee, you are touchy. I didn't know you were that crazy about her." Erv was very fond of Jake even though he always seemed different from his other friends. He knew Jake liked school and sneaked novels

31

from the local library so he could read late at night when everyone else had gone to bed. Maybe he had found a kindred spirit in Ellie.

"Jake, I was here since early this morning to help unhitch the horses and I saw a place in the west hay mow where we could wrestle. Let's go check it out."

As they were leaving the horse stable Jim Cassidy passed them and couldn't seem to help himself as he cockily taunted, "I see I scared the piss out of you already. Why I would guess you're not more than five feet six inches, 140 pounds."

"That's pretty close," Jake replied in his quiet manner, "maybe we should just forget the whole thing since it wouldn't be an even match anyway."

"No way, you little chicken."

Jake had already decided on the strategy of getting Jim to under-estimate him, and he also knew his own anger adrenalin would be pumped up by Cassidy's cocky bravado. Very quietly now, Jake explained to Jim, "We Amish do have certain rules we follow for our wrestling matches." Jake purposely emphasized the implication that he did not in any way consider Jim as being one of them. "I'll let my friend, Erv here explain our rules."

"First of all, this is just a sport we have for fun and second, no one can use any weapons or tools in the match, or try to seriously hurt anyone like knocking out teeth or breaking bones," Erv explained. "You and Jake will be matched up but the other guys will throw their hats on the floor and they will wrestle whoever's hat they pick up after they are mixed up in a pile."

Jake quietly and without looking at Jim said, "I will wrestle you just for fun even though you and I already know it won't be too much of a contest."

"We are all set then," Erv interrupted because he had caught on to Jake's plan of letting Jim think there would be no contest. "We are meeting in the west hay mow then, at about two o'clock. Jake and I will start rounding up the guys."

"Sure thing," Jim yelled back as his back disappeared into the horse stable.

"Hochmutig," Jake muttered with disgust.

"Ya, I know what you mean," Erv added. "I don't think I've ever met anyone so arrogant and full of himself."

"He makes me so mad. Maybe he needs to be brought down a few notches," Jake replied barely above a whisper.

Finally, at about two-thirty, the rest of the boys finished their meals, made their trips to the horse stable, and climbed up the built-in ladder that led through a hole up to the west hay mow. Most of the boys had already piled their coats on top of the loose hay stacked in the mow for the coming winter and were standing in the small area, about eight by ten feet, listening to Jim brag about how he had beaten up a Detroit kid with a baseball bat. Jake was aware that at this point Jim completely misread the silence of the boys for admiration when they were actually hiding their disgust about such violence.

"Arshloch," someone muttered.

Everybody laughed except Jim who demanded, "What are you laughing about? Who said that?" Jim was getting angrier. Erv stepped up to the middle of the circle as the tension grew.

"Alright guys, you all know the rules, but maybe I should remind everyone what they are." Everyone but Jim knew that this was meant only for him because none of them had to be reminded. "Get your hats," Erv continued, "and put them on a pile and then we can draw for wrestling partners, that is, everyone except Jake and Jim since they have agreed to wrestle the last match."

"Kannst gut English spreche," teased someone from the back. Erv just laughed but added that he was speaking English out of respect for Jim who didn't understand their language.

"Joe, would you put the hole cover in place by the ladder so no one gets hurt and we'll spread some fresh straw over the hay to keep from getting so many scratches from the dry hay stalks."

After they spread the straw in the middle of the home-made ring, Johnny, age fourteen, was asked to pick one of the fifteen broad-rimmed black hats from the pile. "Just my luck," he complained when Joe said that the hat was his. Joe was a husky, muscular eighteen-year-old who was even stronger than Jake and considered tall at five feet eleven inches. The only reason Jake could best him in a match was because of his quickness and his ability to keep him pinned for a three count.

"That's not a fair match. Why, Joe could kill that kid," Jim yelled.

Erv then stepped up to Jim and explained, "We wrestle just for fun, you know, just as a sport. We like to win, but it is more important to have fun testing our strength and quickness. Joe will win, of course, but Johnny can show how strong he is anyway."

"Okay, Okay," Jim responded and sat back down on the hay mound shaking his head.

"Let's go Johnny," Erv encouraged, and the first match started.

Johnny rolled up his sleeves. He looked up at Joe's smiling face and said, "Oh, well I might as well get this over with." He walked onto the straw to meet Joe's crouched stance and to everyone's surprise started to talk to Joe. Joe relaxed, stood up out of his crouch, and at that split second Johnny simultaneously grabbed Joe's right arm and pulled back as hard as he could and shot his left foot behind Joe's leg. In one smooth quick move they both went down with Johnny on top.

"Why, you little sneak," Joe said as he started laughing. No matter how hard Johnny tried he could not keep his powerful opponent pinned on his back. Joe purposefully prolonged the bout for a while before he positioned himself on top for the three count.

"You are strong and quick for your age," Joe complimented Johnny. "Also very sneaky," he added as they laughed and shook hands. Johnny glowed from the compliment and still could hardly believe he had flipped Joe onto his back.

While Jake was watching the other bouts he noticed that Jim had left the hay mow and assumed he had gone to relieve himself in the horse stable. Yet he was puzzled because Jim had returned almost immediately, hardly enough time to take care of his personal business. But his attention was now riveted on the next-to-last match, which was lasting a long time because Erv and Joe were so evenly matched neither one could pin the other for a full count keeping both shoulders touching the floor.

Finally, someone suggested they call it a tie and they readily agreed and sat down, exhausted.

"I say it's about time to show you guys a real fight," Jim said with a smirk.

Silence suddenly covered the chatter and Erv got up and tried to lighten the tone with, "Just have a good time, Jim." All eyes were on Jake as he took off his shirt. Erv winked at Jake as he was concerned how quiet he had become, that he might be too serious, too angry.

Jim then made the mistake of taunting, "Come on, you scared?" Jake then joined Jim on the straw and they both went into the crouch, their arms extended and nothing could be heard except the rustling straw under their feet. Jake locked his eyes on Jim's, looking for any slight advantage. At the meal he had noticed that Jim was left-handed. He would try to grab his right hand assuming that was the weaker one. He waited, jerked back each time Jim tried to grab him, knowing Jim would get impatient and eventually give him an advantage. Jim was getting angrier now and lunged toward Jake. In a millisecond Jake grabbed his right arm and in a lightning smooth motion held onto the arm while turning 180 degrees, which lifted Jim off his feet, over Jake's right side, landing on his back with Jake on top boring both knees into Jim's biceps.

"One, two," but Jim got one shoulder up, buckled his legs, and with a heave, threw Jake into the air; but with his innate sense of balance, Jake managed to land back on his feet.

"Way to go Jake," cheers started coming from the wrestlers. "You can do it. Take him again."

Jim had gotten up. His face was red. He was more angry than ever. Clearly he had underestimated Jake. Jake was disappointed. He had wanted to make quick work of Jim; pin him for the full count, get out and go home. Once more they took their positions and again Jake dodged away from Jim's lunges until he sensed the impatience. Jim got careless. He was so worried about his arm that he forgot his right leg's position, which was extended closer to Jake than his arm. With the quickness of a panther Jake dove for the leg, swiveled behind Jim, and lifted him up over his head so that he landed on his back. He followed through all in the same motion and could not stop in time to veer away from the blade. Jim had pulled an army knife from somewhere when he landed on his back that shaved a piece of skin off Jake's right arm. Blood was spurting out. At the same time Jake rolled away, Erv leaped from the side. His right shoe landed on Jim's left wrist, squirting out the knife.

Jake grabbed the knife. Joe pounced from the right side and Jim screamed out in pain. Joe had kneed him in the right shoulder when he landed from four feet away. A deadly silence hung in the air. There was no sound at all except for Erv's enraged, quivering voice.

"You stupid English. You talk so big, but you act like chicken shit. Don't you ever try that again. Get out of here. You're smelling up the place."

Jim climbed down the ladder in a huff taking one last look at Jake who was staring at him to imprint a permanent image he could never forget while Johnny was applying a tourniquet to the bleeding arm. Johnny was scared and furious. "Should we plan to get him?"

"No, just leave him alone. Maybe he's learned his lesson," Jake replied. But he kept his thoughts to himself. There was something sinister about this Jim Cassidy; a smell of evil, a danger worse than fighting dirty. Jake sensed this would not be the last time they would meet.

"You all right?" Erv asked. "I jumped in as soon as I could."

"Ya, I'm okay. The bleeding is beginning to stop. I'm lucky he didn't bite an artery."

"Well, I have to go now to hitch up the horse and I'll see you in two weeks."

"Sure, Erv, see ya," Jake answered. He couldn't wait to go home and be alone with his thoughts about this stranger, the English Amishman. "I wonder where I'm going to see him again?"

Chapter Five

Fish Lake

Jake tugged his bandage to a snug fit and put his shirt back on. The torn shirt tail was just barely long enough to go back into his pants. He pulled his suspenders over his shoulders and decided to wear his suit coat to hide the wrestling damage; climbed down the ladder from the hay mow and headed for the horse stable. There were still a dozen horses lined up and he spotted Nellie, his father's pacer, at the far end, so he left to find out when they would be leaving. As he left the barn there was a line of buggies and impatient horses waiting to leave, but there was some kind of hold up. Jake noticed that at the end of the lane leading to the road Preacher Sam Miller's mare was balking. Sam was in front of the horse pulling on the reins and the harder he pulled the more she balked, stiffening all four legs, making it impossible to move forward.

"The mare maybe thinks she is a mule," a soft feminine voice chuckled right behind Jake.

"Guess so," he said as he turned to see who was there. "Oh, it's you. I thought I recognized your voice. I figured you had already left. Ah, um, ahm, Ellie, I'm glad you're still here because I had wanted to ask if, maybe, perhaps, ah, you might want to do something, well…"

39

"Jake, are you just balking too, or are you a little nervous?" she teased.

"Balking, of course," he retorted and they both laughed, but their eyes locked, her cheeks blushed, his breath shortened.

"I would be happy to do something together next Sunday afternoon since that will be the in between church day."

Jake discreetly brushed her hand and said, "How about if I pick you up a little after dinner, say about one o'clock, and we'll go for a row-boat ride on Fish Lake?"

"I love that idea and I'll make a picnic basket. Oh, I have to go, see you Sunday."

"Bye," Jake softly replied and watched her step up into the buggy, then realized her sisters were already teasing her about her new romance.

He saw his father coming toward the lane from the house adjusting his broad-rimmed black hat and knew they would also be leaving soon. So he made his way to the stable to get Nellie. His heart was still beating fast from talking to Ellie and he was glad to busy himself and hoped his father hadn't seen him asking Ellie for a date. Not that his father would object. Actually, he neither approved nor disapproved; it was just another subject they would never talk about. Jake just knew he and his father would never be able to talk about his girlfriends. His father never asked and he never volunteered. They both pretended as if the matter did not exist.

Nellie was a nervous horse so Jake tried to calm her by talking in a low gentle tone, led her to the buggy, and backed her in between the curved shafts. His father guided the shafts into the leather harness loops, one on each side, and fastened the tugs onto the single tree while Jake took the long bridle reins and single wrapped them around the driver's side buggy post.

Jake sat in the back seat of the double-buggy while his mother joined his father in the front seat. His arm was beginning to hurt from the knife scrapes. He tried to ignore it by reliving the match with that strange Cassidy fellow, but the pain kept getting worse. Remembering Ellie seemed more soothing.

His mother sensed something was wrong, looked back and said, "My you seem very quiet, something wrong?"

Jake was relieved by her sensitivity, yet wished she wouldn't intrude. He wished he could tell them about the wrestling match with the English Amishman and his knife wound, yet he did not want to hear about how hard they work and here he goes and ruins his clothes. At the same time he could not ever tell them about his excitement about Ellie, even though he knew his mother would know anyway, somehow or other with her sensing.

"No, nothing is wrong," he lied, "but I was just thinking if next Sunday I might be able to have Nellie and the single buggy."

"Oh, you gonna have a date, are you?" his mother seemed delighted.

"All I asked was if I could use the buggy?" Jake wished she did not say that in front of his father.

His father saved him from the dating topic by saying, "Sure Jake, you can use the buggy next Sunday. Mom and I weren't planning to go anyplace anyway."

"Thanks, Dad." Deliberately Jake steered them away from questions about why he wanted the buggy so he asked, "Did you see Sam Miller's balker?"

"Wasn't that funny?" his father laughed and added, "Ya, sometimes I'm not sure who's the smartest, Sam or his mare."

"Now Amos, how can you say such a nasty thing about Preacher Miller?" his mother protested and they rode home the rest of the way in silence.

The excitement of brushing Ellie's hand stayed with Jake throughout the week. She did not seem like the other Amish girls. Her witty remark about whether he was also balking or just nervous endeared her to him somehow, in a way he could not understand. He just knew it made him feel intimate, or maybe touched in some personal way. She seemed to know he was nervous, but her tease felt accepting of this knowing.

The first time he saw Ellie was at a Sunday evening social gathering they called a Singing. These socials were often held at the home where the church services had been held during the day. He remembered it was a crisp evening in May and Erv had to talk him into going to the Singing that night instead of going home and curling up with *The Robe*, a book he had checked out of the high school library. Erv remained his friend and tolerated Jake's rebellion of defying his parents and the church by going to high school after the mandatory age of sixteen. While he tolerated this, he still could not understand why Jake was so determined to go to school and he especially seemed dumbfounded that Jake could prefer to go home and read a novel instead of meeting girls at the Singing. Finally, Jake relented and they had arrived after dark finding a crowd of about eighty young folks, ages sixteen and older.

A group of guys were hanging around the horse stable telling off-color jokes and drinking beer they had brought with them. On the way to the house they saw people were milling around outside, some of them necking in the buggies, and eight people were crowded into a blue Oldsmobile with an out-of-state license plate, listening to the radio.

"Can you believe all these people? I don't even know half of them here," Erv gasped with excitement. "Come on Jake, let's go to the house and check out the girls. We'll just pretend we're interested in singing those gospel songs."

"At least the songs are in English and we can sing harmony," Jake replied purposely skirting his interest in meeting new girls.

They had entered through the kitchen door and the huge eat-in kitchen and dining room area were packed with young folks singing "When the Roll is Called Up Yonder, I'll Be There." That was when she had caught his eye. She was standing on the other side of the room under one of the gas lanterns. The bright light shone on her long blond hair parted in the middle. But instead of having pulled it straight back, which was the custom, she had let it hang loosely out of the white see-through cap giving it a soft, sensuous effect. She caught him looking at her and to his surprise, instead of looking away shyly, she smiled and winked at him. Instinctively, Jake looked away. He could not quite believe what happened. "That is just about the most un-Amish thing I've ever seen," he thought, but yet found it strangely appealing.

To his surprise he heard himself saying to Erv, "Let's work our way around to the other side. I have to meet that blond. Do you know her?"

"Hey, I thought you wanted to read a book," Erv teased. "No, I don't think I've ever seen her before."

They moved to the other side of the room, stood behind her for the next song, and then Jake had asked her if she would like to go outside for a little walk so they could meet. She had readily agreed. It was on this brief walk he had first noticed her graceful glide that reminded him more of a pacer than a trotter.

The week, which at times seemed to be a repeat of the Bible story when the sun and time stood still for Moses, finally came to a close and Jake's only worry was whether there would be an available boat for rent at Fish Lake. He wished they would be allowed to have a telephone so he could just call their office and reserve one.

He tried his best to appear casual and nonchalant on Sunday morning, but his mother was cheerful and solicitous and seemed to be showing the excited feelings for both of them. She had only said to have a good time when he left, but he knew that she knew he was very excited about seeing Ellie. Instead of recognizing his excitement he had merely told her to tell his father that he would be home in time to help him with the milking.

As he approached the Hostetler farmhouse he reined Nellie to a slow pace not wanting to appear too eager. Ellie and her whole family, three brothers and five sisters, were sitting on homemade wooden lawn benches in the back lawn that was visible from the road and Jake realized they were eating dinner, their noon meal. He felt a surge of nervousness shoot through him as he turned into the lane, but was very relieved he did not have to meet the whole family as Ellie had seen him coming, and met him with her prepared picnic basket as he drove up. Neither one spoke as he helped her into the buggy while holding onto the reins. She then held the reins while he walked around the back and put the basket into the small lidded wooden trunk.

Nellie picked up speed and they exchanged admiring glances for a quarter mile on the gravel road before Ellie broke the silence.

"I'm so excited you asked me to go for a boat ride, and it's so romantic."

Jake merely nodded and smiled. She was stunningly beautiful in her pale red dress that was fitted snug to her figure. Her Sunday clothes with the extra required layers badly served their intended purpose of hiding her full figure. She had also removed her small white prayer veil, revealing her soft, thick blond hair.

"You still balking?" She teased and they both laughed out loud, startling Nellie.

"Well, I'm just not used to having someone saying so bluntly what they are feeling, like when you said that you were excited and feeling romantic."

"I'm sorry, I did not mean to make you feel uncomfortable..."

"No, no, don't change. It just seems strange to me. It seems so un-Amish and exciting. Okay?"

"I think I know what you mean, but you know in some ways you are not very Amish. It's not very Amish for you to be going to high school. You're already seventeen. But Jake, you know what? I like that. I wish I could go myself."

"So why don't you just do it?" Jake asked.

"Because my father said if I went to high school he would not support me and I certainly could not live in his house."

"You really think he would do that?"

"He would! You don't know him. He was not all too pleased about me going out with you but my mother stood up for me."

"We're almost there now. Haw, Nellie, Haw." Nellie turned left and Jake reined her to the hitching post by the boat shed.

"I'll tie her up and you can get the basket. I see there is still a boat here for rent. I'll go to the office. Back in a bit."

He paid the boatman the two dollars and assured him the boat would be brought in by five o'clock at the latest. He had saved the money this past week by loading broilers for an English neighbor. But so far the way things were turning out, he thought, the money was well spent. He had never had such a good time being with an Amish girl before. She was different, excitingly different.

"Over here, Ellie, we get the dark green." The boat was lying upside down on the edge of the water. Jake had already rolled up his shirt sleeves and tightened his suspenders to his dark grey denim trousers. He removed his black shoes, rolled his trousers up to his knees, and gingerly walked on the wet loam to the boat. He partially straddled the boat for leverage and with one motion was able to right the boat onto its bottom.

"Too bad they don't have a pier here, but this is really just a fisherman's lake," Jake explained to Ellie as he maneuvered the boat into the water to the high dry clump where she was standing. She deftly stepped into the boat, then held the basket while he fitted the oars into their respective slots.

The blue sky was clear except for a few slow-moving clouds that lazily drifted by occasionally shading the sun for a moment or two.

Jake's back was to the sun as they headed east and all that could be heard was the ripple of the boat moving through the dark blue water and the splash of the oars as they rhythmically slapped the surface. Ellie sat relaxed, at peace, her face toward the sun with her eyes closed. Jake watched her face as he rowed and realized he had never even dreamed such beauty could exist. Not even the Katie of his dreams was so angelic and yet so sensuous. The sunlight shone on her head and a soft breeze stroked her golden hair. It seemed to Jake that the sunlight and the breeze were playing, playing with her hair. The breeze would move the strands and the sun would alter its color, back and forth, taking turns, but never the same shape or tint, playing, gently playing.

Jake rowed on, feeling his powerful shoulder muscles at each pull of the oars, and then gradually turned right toward the south end of the small lake by slightly easing up his right arm pull while keeping a steady rhythm. She opened her eyes in the turn away from the direct sunlight and smiled.

"This is wonderfully peaceful Jake, but exciting too. You let me just enjoy the quiet, the sun, the air. The only thing I heard was the water and a faint clip-clop, clop-clip, clop-clop of a horse on the black top far into the distance." Ellie had said this in an almost dream-like way. Then she sat upright from her cozy slouch and with a twinkle in her eye looked steadily into his and coyly insisted, "Where are you taking me Jake?"

Jake's heart skipped a beat but pretended a mere playfulness as he said, "They tell me the water gets very dark and deep at the south end of this lake, over there, by the deep shadows of the woods. That is usually where the fishermen go for their catch, but I noticed we are the only ones on the lake this afternoon."

Ellie interrupted, "But we aren't fishermen so are you my catch or am I yours?"

"Ellie! I did not say anything like that!" Jake protested.

"Oh, but you did, Jake," she teased. "You just have to listen a little. I read this book last week. Some French guy wrote it. Tourner, no, I think it was Tournier. Anyway, he was saying something about symbolism, you know like you think you are only saying one thing, but other things are meant at the same time."

"You mean like when the minister gets up, especially Sam Miller, and gives this whole spiel about how humble he is; how anybody else could do a better job than he, and blah, blah, blah? And yet we know he is about as righteous and arrogant as they come. It's like he uses words to hide the truth. Is that what you mean?"

"Boy, I think you do know what I mean. But why then don't you see what you said about the fishermen? You acted as if our eyes hadn't met, as if they hadn't said anything."

"Oh, that," Jake responded softly. "You're really something, something special. I'm not used to having someone else listen like that, you know like listening to an animal. Sometimes I think animals talk better than people. That's why I just don't like to say much around people. They can be so confusing, but it helps when I listen in that other way."

"Wow, you're so serious, so intense about—"

"I'm sorry, I didn't mean to go on so much..."

"Jake, I liked it; it makes you even more interesting than I realized before," Ellie said gently as she moved forward in the boat and looked into his face while adding he would really enjoy the Tournier book.

Jake stopped rowing, letting the boat drift slowly into the deepening shadows cast by the thick, tall maple leaves on the west bank; shadows that turned the deep dark still water into black ink. He moved forward, his legs straddled her knees, their arms wrapped around, and then their lips touched, at first gently. Then she opened her mouth to him and time and place were no more, only passion. They drifted in timeless age and spaceless sea; in union, neither moving nor standing still, locked into the soul's embrace; the fiery passion held by the gently rocking, drifting boat hidden in the deep shadows.

The boat drifted against a rock at the water's edge. Jake instinctively released Ellie and leaned to his right to keep the boat balanced. "Whoa! Guess that's about as far as we can go. We hit the edge of the bank. I'll move the boat over there where we can step out."

Jake saw she was flushed with excitement and catching her breath, but asked, "You want to go out here? We could picnic here in the clover field."

"I suppose so," she sighed as she stepped out of the boat with the basket. "But I hate hitting edges," she complained and they both laughed as they hugged and laid down in the thick bed of lush green clover.

They kissed for a long time. Her tongue slowly, deliberately, explored his mouth. His excitement could no longer be contained or hidden. Her long skirt bunched up almost to her waist. She felt his need. He reached to stroke her soft smooth thigh and turned his head toward her blue eyes filled with tears.

Shocked, Jake sat up. "What's the matter?" he asked gently. "What's wrong?" he urged as he cradled her in his arms.

She couldn't talk. Her tears turned to sobs. She let him hold her for a long time as he held her tight and gently rocked the little child within her.

Suddenly Ellie leaped up and ran off into the clover field. Jake ran after her. By the time he caught up with her she was laughing.

"Ellie, Ellie, what got into you? What are you doing?"

"Oh, nothing. Sorry I cried. Didn't mean to spoil our fun. Let's go have our picnic."

Jake worried. He could not let go of what happened so easily. "Ellie, just a minute ago you were crying like a little child, like someone who was either very scared or very, very hurt. What happened? Were you scared?"

"Stop pestering me. Forget it, I'm not going to talk about it. Come on, let's just have fun," she added looking right into his eyes in dead earnest.

Jake saw that look, a look of warning. "Back off," her eyes flashed like the eyes of an angry dog. This was a look Jake understood.

"Race you back to the basket," Ellie yelled over her shoulder as she took off and just barely won the thirty-yard foot race.

"Boy, you can run," Jake said as he joined her at the basket. Her vivacious mood and playfulness once more captured him. He pushed the crying spell to the back of his mind. He told himself she would explain someday when she was good and ready.

Chapter Six

Birth

The next morning Jake had awakened early and was lying in bed reliving and savoring every detail of being with Ellie. He was in love. He had never felt so deeply about a girl. Deep in his heart he knew Ellie was his for life. They had rowed back to the buggy in silence flowing in a love and perfect communion that words could only diminish. The sun had descended to about the five o'clock point and danced its reddish rays playfully on the water except where the long shadows of the trees announced the ending of the day. The color of the reds and oranges glanced off her blue eyes and tinted her ruffled blond hair. That was all he saw. The sun, the rays in the water, the rippling shadows, and her eyes holding him, all of him. They didn't talk. Ellie's crying spell was all but forgotten. It was not mentioned again.

Not until they were snuggled in the buggy did she ask him about his arm. She had taken his hand in hers and gently asked, "Jake, how did you scrape your arm?"

"Just from a little horseplay with the boys after church last week," he replied.

"Just from a little horseplay," she laughed. "Must have been quite a horse!"

Jake laughed with her but then decided to tell her about Jim Cassidy and the wrestling, how he had been challenged by Jim's rude bragging, the knifing, and about his suspicions of the strange English dressed in Amish clothes.

Ellie had simply replied, "Maybe you paid too much attention to his words. Next time you see him listen to him like you listen to animals."

"But I did, sort of, but I didn't want to say too much to Erv because he always kids me about that. I think you're right, though," he had added.

To his surprise he heard footsteps coming up the stairs and could tell from the sound that his father was already up even though he had just heard the clock from the living room strike only four times.

"Jake," he called gently.

His father was hard to figure. Sometimes he could be so harsh and yet at other times be gentle like now, but there was also a faint worry laced in the tone.

"It's still pitch dark out. Is something wrong?" Jake asked.

"I know it's early but I heard a deep moan coming from the cow barn. I think it's one of the heifers trying to give birth."

"Okay, I'll be there right away."

"I'll take the kerosene light out to the barn. You bring the gas lantern because we will need good lighting, but you may have to put some gas in it first."

"Ya, I know how to get all that. I'll be there in no time," Jake said, but he noticed that he wasn't as irritated as usual with his father's methodical instructions. He stayed under the sheets until he heard his father's steps creaking the wooden stairs in order to hide his erection. Then he jumped out of bed, grabbed his short-sleeved, pale blue shirt, and his gray denim pants, which were hanging on the bed post. He had put them there the night before, as he always did, with his heavy work shoes and socks also at the ready.

His older brother had given him the idea for this routine and they used to compete who could get dressed the fastest. Joe always beat him. Joe beat him in everything. He was seven years older than Jake and while he often teased him unmercifully, he took pains to teach Jake almost everything he knew, from skinning muskrats to tying a slip knot. Joe was short and stocky and the most powerfully built of the two. He had made such a reputation as a wrestler that Jake felt compelled to follow suit. Right now he longed for Joe to be there to help.

When he got to the barn with the gas lantern his father had already spread clean straw around Hazel who was lying on her side breathing loud and heavy. Her rear legs were spread wide, her tail was raised, and something was hanging out of her vagina. Jake hung the lantern onto a ceiling hook and went closer. His stomach was feeling queasy. His father was crouched down stroking Hazel's neck and talking in low soothing tones. Jake looked more closely and realized the thing he had seen hanging out of Hazel was a calf's leg. It looked like a wet crooked stick with the tip pointed at the heifer's stomach. "Oh, no," he blurted out, "that's the hind leg, no wonder it doesn't come out."

"That's right. Now what we have to do," his father continued in a calm tone that controlled his worry, "I want you to run to the house and bring out a bucket of hot water. Then go to the buggy shed and bring the quarter-inch rope. While you do that I will try to get both hind legs out so we can pull as Hazel pushes."

Jake was only too glad to get out of the barn for some air. His stomach felt weak. The sight of the heifer lying exhausted on her side with her head flat on the floor and moaning made him shiver all the way through. He wished he was not so sensitive and squeamish. It didn't seem becoming to an Amish farmer. "I bet Joe wouldn't be bothered like this," he thought.

When he returned with the water and the rope, his father had already managed to pull the other hind leg out. They tied the rope around both legs and waited for the next contraction to begin. When it came Hazel let out such a loud moan it startled Jake so much he forgot to pull on the rope.

"Come on Joe, you've got to pull harder and at the right time."

"I know, I'll get it," Jake quickly responded, ignoring being called by his brother's name, but he felt somehow honored.

They worked together, the three of them, for another whole hour before they finally were able to push-pull the calf out. Hazel just lay there exhausted and the wet brown calf had trouble breathing. Jake felt like he was going to faint or throw up, he was not even sure which, but he held on by wiping off the calf with a dry gunny sack while his father used short stalks of straw to clean out the nostrils. Finally she started breathing easier when another deep groan came from the heifer.

"Not again," Jake said exasperated.

His father quickly said, "Don't worry, she still needs to get rid of her afterbirth. If she can do that yet, then she will be okay."

Just then the groan and contraction were over and the gooey, sloshy, sickening blob of bloody and purplish afterbirth came out with a swoosh onto the cement floor, mixing with the lime and straw. Jake felt his stomach churn. He simply turned and left, went to the hay mow and tried to think of anything but the scene he just witnessed. He tried to think of Ellie, then Cassidy, and Joe. Gradually his stomach settled and his fainting feeling subsided. How long he was up there, he didn't know. But he was glad his father did not ask him where he was when he got back.

Chapter Seven

Hog Pen

Jake and his father proceeded with the morning farm chores with each one having their own routines. His father had always taken pride in efficiency so always insisted each one had specific tasks. After the calf was born Jake automatically went up into the hay mow to fork the dry alfalfa hay down the hole that dropped into a pile in front of the cow stanchions. Then he did the same from the opposite mow for the horses while his father proportioned the right amount of oats and corn for the horses and doled out the mash mixed with molasses for the cows.

His father then swept the milking stable and sprinkled fresh lime on the cement floor while Jake slopped the hogs and fed them corn. They finished about the same time and together went to the milk house to get the galvanized milk pails and the ten-gallon cans for the milking. They pushed the heavy steel-wheeled cart together in silence except for his father's low humming.

No matter how fast and hard Jake worked his stomach would not let him forget the scene of the brown swiss heifer lying on her side, in pain, and spewing out the bloody, purplish afterbirth. His father was pleased. Hazel and her calf were saved. Not until they had carted the milk to the milk house and lifted the two full milk cans into the cold water tank to keep it cool did his father begin his routine of spelling out the work for the day.

"Right after breakfast we'll haul the manure out of the hog pen. That will take us to dinner time. Since the corn is too tall to cultivate anymore and the haying is done, I want you to start trimming the walnut tree we cut down last week. When you start loading manure I will go to the tool shed and sharpen the axes for you. I figure you will have all afternoon, right after dinner, to get a good start on that tree. Stop about half past five so we have plenty of time to do the chores. With the new calf and heifer there is going to be a little more work."

Jake had listened and nodded. Long ago he had learned to take the instructions in silence. He showed neither that he hated nothing more than cleaning the hog pen nor that he was excited to hone his skill with the axe. He just hoped there would be no more than three manure spreader loads in the pen. Hog manure had a stench just as strong as chicken droppings so that his clothes had to be washed promptly. He determined that he would work at a feverish pitch so by noon that job would be finished so he could chop wood all afternoon.

Right after a hearty breakfast of eggs over easy, pancakes, hash browns, and fried mush with syrup, Jake went to his room and changed his gray denim pants for an older patched one with strong leather suspenders he wore for pitching manure. Then he went to the basement and found an old pair of Joe's rubber boots, pulled them over his work shoes, stuffed his pantlegs into the boots that almost reached up to his knees, and buckled the six metal clasps. Now he was ready to harness up his favorite team, Cap and Carl.

"Cap," was short for captain. He was clearly the team's leader. He was the first to respond to Jake's signals and Carl would reluctantly follow. He started with Cap, talking gently as he worked. With the dull toothed metal scraper in his right hand and the hairbrush in his left he alternated his strokes in a rhythmical right-left, right-left motion, removing any loose hair. "Now, doesn't that feel better, Cap? Let me just get this loose fuzz off your sides. Whoa now, hold still, almost done." Cap turned his head back from the stanchion. "Don't worry, Cap. You won't have to work hard today. Just pull the spreader. You think you have it hard. I'm the one with the hard work, fork-pitching that heavy smelly stuff. Easy Cap, here we go." Jake had taken the horse collar off the hook, spread the top, slipped it up from the bottom onto the thin part of the neck right behind the head, then slid it toward the shoulders for a snug fit. "Now for the hardest part, Cap. Whoa, hold still." In one smooth motion Jake flipped the rest of the harness onto Cap's back, buckled the banes into the collar grooves and fastened the belly band.

"Okay, Carl, your turn," Jake approached knowing Carl would not be as cooperative as Cap. Carl mainly ignored Jake and munched his hay in the manger that was left from the morning's feeding. But this time Carl did not give any trouble until Jake was bridling him and he refused to open his mouth for the snaffle bit. Jake then led both of the horses out of the barn gripping the bridle reins and led them to the manure spreader. He backed the team to the spreader so that they straddled the tongue, one on each side, snapped the steel ring attached at the end of the tongue onto the yoke, and fastened the tugs onto the doubletree. He took the check reins, climbed up to the metal seat atop the front end of the spreader and signaled giddy up. Cap started. Carl didn't, until the second signal.

They drove around the barn to the hog house. "Haw," Jake signaled as he tugged the left check rein. Cap turned left and Carl followed. His father had already cleared the pen of hogs so Jake could drive the spreader right to the open door for loading.

"See you're all set up," his father said, "I'll go sharpen the axes now." As he was leaving he added, "I brought the long-handled shovel and four-pronged fork out for this."

"Ya, okay," Jake replied keeping his sarcastic remark in check. He felt like saying, "You think I'm dumb? I know you can't use a hay fork for this shit."

It was late August. A hot day with very little breeze. The stench was already beginning to sting his nostrils. He guessed the manure was six inches deep, more or less, throughout the fifteen by thirty foot shed. Even though they bedded the pen twice a day with bales of straw there was almost no straw visible. Twenty-five pigs with their pointed little feet romping around the pen changed the straw into a soup of feces, giving it just enough texture so most of it could be forked instead of shoveled.

"Boy, I hate this!" He opened the north door hoping any breeze might help. His nose was stinging. He was getting more and more angry. He opened his shirt but kept it on to protect his shoulders from the leather suspenders and began to attack the manure, loading it as fast as his back could take it. At places the manure was packed so hard he had to use the fork as a leverage by sticking the prongs into the pile, placing the handle on his knee, and pushing down on the handle without breaking it. He was working at a furious pace and had almost filled the spreader when his father stuck his head into the door.

"Jake, I'm going to the mill. Be back by noon dinner." That's when he noticed what Jake had already done. "For Pete's sake, don't try to get this all done in a couple hours. There may be three full loads in here."

"Okay, okay," Jake tried to sound compliant. "But why doesn't he help with this! Sure wish Joe were here," he thought. "In a month I'll be back in high school. That will be so easy compared to this." His father had relented and agreed to let Jake finish high school over the furious protests of his mother. For this Jake also thanked his brother Joe for breaking the way. Joe had been the first to rebel by going to school past his sixteenth birthday. Jake had then followed suit.

School was like a vacation for him and he thought it humorous when the English boys complained about school being too much work while he couldn't seem to get enough books. He then remembered he wanted to ask Ellie for the book she had mentioned on the boat and entertained himself reliving their experience as he worked.

He still felt some kind of badness, some guilt about what he and Ellie had done yesterday. "Why do I feel bad? Just because I did something I wasn't 'supposed' to do? The love and peace I felt at the time was real, so why feel bad now. Or was there something about Ellie; she did seem a bit strange, a bit frightened and driven at one point when her eyes got that far away, distant look. But then her eyes returned to me and she was more passionate than before. Why did she cry?"

Nothing came clear to him, but he did know that the badness he felt now was different from the feeling he had after the walk in the woods with Polly. That time he felt used, dirtied, and angry. He had just turned sixteen. She had asked him to go on a walk with her into the woods a quarter of a mile from her house. She was a dark brunette in long braids and in that last year had developed a woman's figure. Jake had known her since the third grade and in their childhood had played ball and tag games. She had given him cues of her interest in him, but he had pretended not to notice. The sun had already set that late fall but it wasn't dark yet when they strolled the dirt lane back to the woods. She said she wanted to show him the water spring that fed the creek that wound through the back of their farm. She chattered about the last Singing she had attended, the people she had met, a new dress her aunt was sewing, but Jake sensed her heart was not into anything she was saying. She was slightly built, almost his height, with long thin legs that she kept showing him by whirling around so that her long skirt showed them off.

Jake felt his body respond and he did not want to hurt her feelings. But before he could understand what he really felt about her they had entered the dusky woods. Polly had thrown her arms around him and kissed him on the mouth. Their lust took over. She removed her panties, put her arms around his neck, and as she wrapped her legs around him, he entered while still standing upright.

He never did see the artesian spring. She had talked on the way back how she wanted him to be her boyfriend, to take her to the Singings and he had listened feeling more and more angry, used, and bad.

Yet, at the same time he sensed her deep desperation and what felt like a pit of sadness that could swallow her up at any time.

But what he said was, "Polly, that was fun back there in the woods. But, I don't feel right about it. It feels like sin, like something bad."

"Oh, don't be so sensitive, Jake. You like me don't you?" she had asked.

He had just smiled not daring to say he did not think so. Three weeks later they ran into each other at a Singing and she insisted they had to talk. Reluctantly he agreed to meet her out by his buggy.

"Jake, I'm worried."

Jake waited silently for her to go on, fidgeting with his shoe on the gravel.

"I might be pregnant. It's been too long."

Jake broke out in a cold sweat, but he could only quietly muster, "Polly, for both of our sakes, I sure hope not."

She tried to cry on his shoulder. He turned and left without saying another word and headed for his horse and buggy. On the way home he tried to pray. Asking for forgiveness brought no relief and the next two weeks he planned how he could have a hunting accident with his twenty-two-caliber rifle; for he knew he could never live with Polly just as he knew he would be ostracized for life if he did not marry her. Finishing high school would be out of the question and his secret dream of going on to college once he was twenty-one would be shattered. Relegated to the farm? An Amish farmer; the rest of his life? He could not stand the thought!

"Jake, it's time for dinner, it's already twelve-thirty," his mother said. She had walked out to the hog pen.

"I forgot to look at the sun; didn't realize what time it was. I'm just finishing up. Would it be okay if I spread the last load first? That way I can clean up and won't have to do it twice."

"Alright, I'll keep the food warm. Maybe by then your father will be home from the mill too," his mother replied.

He took out the third load and spread the manure on the back pasture and said a silent prayer. He thanked God for two things; that Polly had not conceived, and for Ellie. Then he unhitched the team, watered and fed them, and went in for dinner. He washed up in the basement. His mother had prepared a small tub of hot water, lava soap, and a washcloth for that purpose; something she always did to protect the house on those days the men hauled manure.

Chapter Eight
The Visit

After dinner Jake followed his father out to the west lawn for their usual midday rest under the walnut tree. The sun was bright and hot but a slight breeze wafted through the shade. They each found a shady spot several yards apart; his father on his back and Jake on his stomach.

Frisky, Jake's black and white, short-tailed rat terrier, playfully romped back and forth begging to play. Jake's back and shoulders ached from pitching manure. He tried to ignore him by burying his head in his arms. Frisky wasn't going to be denied. He stuck his cool nose on Jake's cheek and when that didn't work, he stood on his short hind legs and pawed Jake's back which finally tickled him in to action. So he picked up several walnuts that retained their bitter green husks and half-heartedly threw them for fetching.

His father shifted his position. He leaned on his right elbow to watch when Jake heard him chuckle.

"Remember that time when your sister Sarah was napping out here and you had Frisky jump on her stomach, and she screamed like a bantam?"

"Yeah." Jake chuckled with him. He also missed Sarah, and Joe too, especially Joe. But he still had Frisky. He sat up so his back was toward his father and stopped throwing the walnuts. Frisky ran up to him wagging his short little tail as fast as he could, eagerly looking for the next lob. When it did not come he put his front paws on Jake's knee and looked straight into his face as if asking what the matter was. Jake answered him by gently stroking the underside of his neck with his right hand. Frisky responded by lying down on his side with his head on one knee and licked Jake's left hand. Frisky licked. Jake stroked. The familiar bothersome lump rose in his throat. He tried not to remember but it was no use. Even though he had not seen the accident he could instantaneously see the sleek long red Buick barreling down route five and crashing into the buggy from the rear. There was nothing Joe could have done.

"Well, it's about time I guess," his father said as he stood up. "I looked at the hog pen and saw you finished that job. You can go ahead and get started on that old walnut tree. The axes are by the flint stone in the shed. I'll go ahead and bed down the pen with fresh straw."

"Ya, okay," Jake replied.

"Just remember to have the right position when you use the axe. You know how they can glance off and break a leg."

"I'll be careful," Jake called back over his shoulder and kept on walking toward the tool shed, not wanting to hear any more instructions and making sure his father could not see his wet cheek.

Frisky still wanted to play and on the walk to the old tree ran ahead of Jake, then back to him, back and forth, back and forth, as if he thought they were going rabbit hunting.

"Frisky, we're not going hunting, come here. Come here! Look at this. This is not a gun. It's an axe. Smell it. That's right, see."

The cut black walnut tree was lying in a small wheat field beside the gravel road where it crashed several weeks ago. Jake and his father hand-sawed the tree using the two-man eight foot saw with a ten-inch handle on each end. First his father had chipped through the half-inch bark with an axe about three feet from the ground on the north side of the tree. Sawing from this side was crucial after determining that the shape

62

and weight of the tall hundred-foot tree would fall due south away from the road. The chipped notch then made it easier to start the sawing.

It had taken almost two hours to saw the three-foot diameter trunk. Jake had been exhausted because it was new work he had not yet mastered. They stood at each end of the horizontally held saw and gripped the vertical wooden handles and began the rhythmical pull-follow, pull-follow motion.

His father had become exasperated. "Don't push when it's my turn to pull. Never push, just follow the saw. Keep your hands on the handle on the follow through, then pull the saw toward you."

When Joe was still at home Jake had watched them use a two-man saw and it had looked easy then. Now it seemed so complicated. His feet had to be positioned just the right distance from the saw to allow a free arm movement to pull then follow, back and forth. If he pushed during the follow through the saw buckled. If he pulled to hard the synchronized rhythm faltered. Then his father had said, "Let the saw do the work, you just pull."

Jake picked up the single-edged axe and began trimming the smaller branches. Frisky was resting in the shade, puffing, his red tongue hanging out. He had been chasing rabbits, but his short little legs could not keep up the pace. His specialty was killing rats from the corn bin, not chasing rabbits. He was quick, not fast.

It took full concentration to swing the axe, making sure he was always in the right position in relation to the branch being cut and keeping a smooth rhythm to ensure each blow hit the exact same spot as the preceding one. This made the work more efficient. He could still hear his father's voice repeating over and over, "Hit the same spot and let the axe do the work, let the axe do the work." After an hour of this his lower back muscles pained for a break so Jake sat down on one of the large uncut limbs. He could feel the welling up again and knew he couldn't keep it down anymore. It was almost three years ago Joe was found dead lying in the ditch beside the splintered buggy.

He could feel the storm coming. He held his head with both hands, and as he fought back the tears the lump in his throat grew into a fierce headache. Frisky ran over, stood on his hind legs, and reached up to lick Jake's face. Jake slid off the log, sat on the ground with his back leaning against the limb and sobbed with his forehead buried in Frisky's soft stubby fur. He held onto Frisky for a long time.

That Monday morning, three years ago, he had awakened in an empty bed. Joe wasn't there. Jake thought nothing of it at the time thinking Joe had risen early. When he was walking to the barn with his father it was still dark and a cold March wind was blowing, he asked, "Where's Joe? He was already up when I woke up."

His father had merely replied, "I didn't see him, I figured he was still in bed since he doesn't have to get up this early to work in that trailer factory."

They had both seen the car with its bright headlights coming from the west on the gravel road kicking up a cloud of dust. To their surprise it was an Indiana State Trooper that drove into their lane. A tall uniformed man got out and told them there had been a very bad car and buggy accident and wondered if this was the Amos Mast home.

His father had gone with the trooper in his car and Jake had to do the chores by himself since his father did not come home for a long time. All through the morning work Jake feared the worst, but kept telling himself the policeman had not said anybody was killed.

The next day an English neighbor had brought them a copy of the *LaGrange News* that headlined the accident along with a photograph of the strewn wreckage showing the splintered wood of the buggy frame. One of the wheels was lying flat on the ground about fifteen feet away still intact; the others were broken into small pieces with the steel rims gnarled and twisted. Reddy, Joe's driving horse, was lying on her right side with a broken rear leg. She was holding up her head trying to get up.

Beside the black curtain flaps, still partially attached to the upper buggy frame, lay a still figure covered with a brown army blanket.

The paper had quoted the Chicago driver of the Buick as saying, "It was a little after midnight. I was going slow, only about fifty miles an hour because I'm not familiar with the road. I came around the curve. I never saw any taillights." Later he had expressed, "I feel very bad about this, but maybe the Amish should learn to stay off our highways."

Remembering "our highways" infuriated Jake so he picked up his axe and went back to trimming the fallen tree. Soon he was streaming with perspiration as he furiously attacked the tree using the double-edged axe on the larger limbs. He kept up this pace until it was time for evening chores.

His father had already prepared the stable for milking and together they worked, mostly in silence. Jake was glad for this so he could work and remember. Joe had reached twenty-one so he had become of age. He no longer had to give his parents the money he earned at the mobile home factory or stay at home to work the farm. He was free to start his own life. He had shared with Jake his dream of going on to college once he was of age and that he probably would not stay Amish. Jake had kept this secret, partly to protect his brother and partly to protect himself because he did not want the church elders to pressure his parents into making him drop out of high school.

They had just finished the chores except for feeding the newborn calf with the teat-bucket when they heard horse hooves and buggy wheels crunching on the gravel lane.

"I wonder who that might be," his father said. "I wasn't expecting anybody. You finish the calf, I'll go see who it is."

After a few minutes his father returned, he looked worried. "You weren't expecting anybody, were you?"

"No," Jake replied. "Why, who is here?"

"Bishop John Bontrager and Preacher Sam Miller are here. They want to talk to you."

Jake's heart sank as he muttered, "Whatever for?" and walked out to the buggy where the ministers were waiting. He steeled himself by trying to act casual, unconcerned, with a friendly "Vie gehts?" while purposely not inviting them in.

"Vell, wie bist du?" Sam was the first to reply.

Bishop John did not bother with the greetings, but explained the purpose of their visit. "We have known for some time now that you are still in high school even though we had asked you not to do that. We've talked to your father a number of times about this, but it doesn't seem to do any good. Hasn't he talked to you about this?"

"Ah, ah sure," Jake lied to protect his father, for only at that moment did he realize that his father had been taking some heat for his being in high school.

"You know the Scriptures say to honor thy father and thy mother and obey them, so you know then that you are in sin, yes?"

"Guess I have to think about that," Jake quietly evaded.

Bishop John kept pressing, "There are other things we have heard; that you wear English clothes to school and that you comb your hair in a worldly fashion with a part on the side. One of the brothers told us he saw you and at first did not even know who you were; that you didn't look Amish at all. What have you to say for yourself?"

"I don't know who that brother was, but I cannot deny what you've said," Jake responded. "I have been reading and studying the Bible. The way I understand it the Bible says what's in a man's heart is very important. It says very little about how to dress except to be modest."

Sam Miller blurted out, "So you are a minister? You can interpret the Scriptures? Why, you're nothing but a boy."

Silence hung in the air for what seemed like an eternity until the bishop said whoa to their horse which began pawing his front foot, eager to get moving. Then he addressed Jake once more saying, "I am afraid for your soul. It is my duty to warn you. You don't obey your father. That science you study in school is taking you away from the Scriptures, and now to hear you wear worldly clothes. Jake, you are going down a dangerous road, the road to hell. After all, you do remember your baptismal vows, yes?"

Jake stood still looking down to hide his rage. He wished this was just a bad dream. He felt more and more angry.

The bishop mistook Jake's posture as submission. In his gentle tone the bishop pleaded, "Jake, can I count on you to change your ways?"

Jake replied, "I will give the warning very serious thought."

Bishop John noted the noncommittal response and added, "Jake, we are going to go now. We'll be praying for you, but just remember your brother Joe also went to high school. Some say he might even have wanted to leave the Amish and go to college. The Bible says whatsoever a man soweth, that he shall also reap."

In fury Jake stood there in the lane as the buggy turned onto the road wishing he could scream, "You flat-earth dummy! Hope you get hit by a car! Then we'll see how you twist the Scriptures."

Chapter Nine

Honeyville

The day finally ended with the customary evening prayer. Jake's mother brought the *German Prayer Book* into the living room and handed it to his father, and without speaking the three of them knelt by their chairs. His father moved closer to the kerosene lamp and began to read the prayer out loud. Jake rested his head in his tired arms and all was quiet, but the lulling sounds of his father's soft Germanic sing-song reading and the tick-tock, tick-tock of the Seth Thomas.

During supper his mother seemed bothered by Jake's silence. She had tried to probe what the ministers had wanted and he had evaded as much as possible by saying only that they talked to him about his hair being cut too short. She knew there was more, but eventually offered that he was probably just exhausted from such a long, hard day of work. Since there was truth in her explanation he let the lie stand and so his silent rage at her beloved bishop remained secret and intact. Another part of him wanted to scream out his real feelings; that the preacher was not only stupid but also mean, a genuine horse's ass to imply that Joe was killed as a divine punishment for going to high school and wanting to leave the Amish. He was getting furious all over again, which was interrupted by his father's "amen."

He got up, bade a quick good night, and went to his room upstairs. While he was fatigued and sore, especially around his shoulders and back, he could not go to sleep. What was bothering him so much? He knew he was angry at the bishop. But was there something else? If he really believed John Bontrager was stupid and mean why couldn't he get to sleep? Could the bishop possibly be right? Would God punish him for leaving the group? By killing his brother? Was this really like Sodom and Gomorrah where populations were destroyed for turning their backs on God? Another Nineveh? But in high school there were many other kinds of Christians. They certainly were not Amish. Why weren't they wiped out by the Almighty's wrath?

His thoughts went to going back to school. This was exciting and Labor Day was only a week away. He was more determined than ever to graduate. Would they excommunicate him? Shun him for life? He'd take the chance, yes, that is what he would do. He knelt beside his bed to pray. The wooden floor felt hard on his knees and the hot night air hung in the room heavy and still. "Dear Father in Heaven," he whispered. "Help me know the way, the right way for me. I read the Bible, I look in my heart, and what I'm doing I think is right. So why does it feel so wrong? Please dear God help me know what is right, and help me feel this." He waited, in the still, heavy silence. Even in the hot heavy air he felt his skin chill. He felt so alone, forsaken. Even God turned away, or maybe was no longer interested. Was He ever there? He climbed into bed and cried himself to sleep.

In the morning he woke up with a frightening dream about walking in their woods late at night. The night was pitch black with no moon or stars shining through the clouds. He was carrying his rifle and slinking barefoot weaving in and out of the trees and thick brush when he heard a rustle to his right. Instinctively he crouched, raised the gun and turned, all in one motion and before him glinted the long white fangs of a huge black dog ready to spring. He pulled the trigger and as the shot rang out the dog's snout flattened into the form of a face that laughed derisively in the voice of Jim Cassidy.

He got up, went to the bathroom and wiped off his cold sweat with a towel and forgot the dream by the time he was dressed to start the morning milking. Not until he was on his way to the barn and Frisky romped toward him did he remember the fanged snout of his dream, and Cassidy. "Why," the questions kept repeating throughout the morning, "was the ferocious dog also Jim Cassidy? Why would a guy like that want to join the Amish? Why would anybody? Does he think this life was easy? Or simple?"

On the way to the milk house his father began the ritual of laying out the work plans he had for the day and to Jake's surprise, right after breakfast the two of them were going to Honeyville, the little village with four stores. Jake wondered to himself, "why Honeyville?" when they did most of their shopping in Topeka, but he did not interrupt. "I need some windowpanes for the chicken house and three-penny nails. After we do this at the hardware store then we could eat at the diner." What sounded like the beginning of an afterthought, his father quietly added without looking at him, "You can also go to the Yoder store to buy some school clothes while I'm at the hardware."

Jake's heart leaped and he felt like hugging his father, but instead he coolly replied, "Okay." But his excitement and appreciation showed in his friendly offer to groom and harness Nellie right after breakfast. They understood each other perfectly, but what was understood was better left implied. They both knew his father was really saying that he was not going to keep Jake home from high school; that Jake had implicit permission to buy English clothes from the Mennonite store, and that he could be in the store by himself so that his father would not be seen buying them.

On the long ride to Honeyville Jake wished he could thank his father outright but decided not to push his luck. He was wondering how he might show his appreciation indirectly when to his surprise, his father directly asked him what the ministers had wanted to talk to him about. With a slight smirk and chuckle he asked, "So what did Sam and John have to say last night?"

Jake was taken aback. The way his father asked the question he realized an attitude that implied his father either did not think too highly of the ministers or probably did not agree with them, or maybe both. His hesitation in responding was misread by his father who quietly added, "Guess that's between you and them."

"They wanted me to promise I would quit going to high school," Jake answered as he realized that his father's silence all those years hid what he really felt and thought. He struggled with telling his father that someone told the bishop about the English clothes, but was afraid his father might change his mind about letting him go to the store. So instead he added, "John says he's worried about me studying science and this could lead me away from God and the Amish. But then he said the meanest thing, something about what we sow, we will reap and so much as said that's what happened to Joe."

"Huh," was all his father said, but Jake could tell he was angry as he slapped a rein on Nellie's rump speeding the pacer to a fast clip. "What else did they say?"

"Well, I didn't want to say this, but they also said a brother had seen me last spring in English clothes coming home from school and that I did not look at all Amish."

They rode in silence for a while, lost in their own thoughts. The sky clouded over and a slight drizzle began. Nellie slowed to a walk while they undid the side curtains and snapped them down to keep the rain out. The drizzle was light so they kept the storm front open. If it rained harder they would close this framed window with slots for the check reins. They left the gravel road and turned onto the black top leading to town, and whenever they saw a car coming from the rear his father would pull Nellie off the pavement and on the shoulder until the car passed.

Jake knew they were both nervous about being on this road with cars buzzing by so he offered, "I'll keep an eye on the rear and tell you when a car is coming." He shifted his position so he could look out the three-by-six inch window in the back curtain to watch for cars.

"Buggies don't really belong on these highways, do they? Everything changed so fast. But, you know," his father continued, "my father tells me that in his younger days there was not that much difference between the Amish and other people. Most of the men wore beards, there were only a few cars, and also, the clothes they wore were pretty much the same. My father says the more time passed the stranger the Amish became until today, eighty years later, they look queer to the rest of the world. Sometimes I think they are so tradition-minded, but don't know it's just recent history."

Jake had never heard his father talk like this, but he wanted more so he asked, "Why do you think this happened to the Amish?"

"I don't know, but sometimes I wonder if it's because they don't read and so they don't really think and so they seem to get more and more narrow all the time."

His father stopped talking. Jake longed for more. He kept quiet hoping his father would continue. He had never heard him say what he really felt. To his surprise he continued.

In a quiet husky voice came, "You know, Joe was a good boy. And smart. And so are you."

There was silence. A lump formed in Jake's throat; tears came to his eyes. His father looked straight ahead, but tears rolled down his cheeks into his black and graying beard. It was the first time Jake had seen his father cry. Nellie walked pulling them through the rain as the two of them cried together, in silence.

Chapter Ten

School

The long-awaited day finally came. The first day of school. It was a warm sunny September morning. Jake and his father had finished the milking early and although nothing was said, Jake knew his father was aware of his excitement about getting back to school.

After breakfast he had gone up to his room to change into his school clothes and lingered until he saw the light blue Ford turn into the circular driveway. Don Kemp, another senior, had agreed to take Jake to and from school. "For three bucks a week to help with the gas," he had said, "I'll be glad to give you a ride." Jake liked Don and his friendly outgoing manner.

Jake ran down the stairs and as he opened the back door his mother stood there looking angry and disapproving, muttering something about his fancy clothes. Jake knew this would happen, but was glad he had lingered upstairs for he did not want to start his first day trying to console his mother.

Now that he knew that his father was not actively going to interfere with his going to school or wearing English clothes, he hoped it would just be a matter of time that his mother could also accept the changes.

After all, what could she do? As an Amish woman she certainly could not leave her husband or her family. The shame would be more than anyone could bear. Besides, he was quite sure she would not shun him like her brothers and sisters did to her ever since they had moved to a more liberal Amish district.

Many times Jake had found his mother sitting alone in the living room crying and once on a rainy Sunday afternoon he asked her, "What is the matter?"

She replied, "I'm worried, just worried."

"What are you worried about?"

The gentle question made the tears flow freely. She wiped her nose with her white handkerchief and kept looking out the east window. He sensed her deep sorrow and pain and sat down on his heels beside her wooden rocker, put his right hand on her left arm and looked out the window with her, listening to her rocking chair creaking rhythmically on the hardwood floor. All else was quiet except for the gentle rain pattering on the eaves and the tick-tock, tick-tock of the old wooden clock as the pendulum swung endlessly back and forth.

She broke the silence with, "My brother Sam gave me this handkerchief. What was it, maybe three, four years ago? See, it even has an M for Mary sewn on it."

Jake knew then she was crying about missing her brothers and sisters who seldom came to visit since the shunning. And even when they did visit they would not eat at the same table for fear of being banned by the rest of the brotherhood of her hometown church district. He merely said, "You're missing your brother Sam, aren't you?"

"Yes," she said in a whisper as she fought back her tears. "It's not right. It just doesn't seem right. I did not leave the Amish. If we left the Amish, well, then I could understand it, them shunning me, not eating with me and all that. But this just isn't right. Es ist nit recht," she kept repeating over and over, shaking her head, holding her handkerchief over her eyes.

"Mom, it isn't right, or even Christian," Jake had tried to soothe her. "Our Amish don't shun Sarah. She joined the Ohio Amish. The Amish group you came from are so arrogant."

"But they are the ones who accuse us of being too 'hochmutig,' too worldly, not humble," she protested.

"So, they don't make any sense," Jake said as he turned to go. He heard Don beep his horn and as he ran to the car he sincerely hoped this would not be too difficult for his mother, that his father could help her adjust to the changes he sensed were yet to come. "The bishop was probably right," he thought, "that getting education and staying Amish was like trying to mix water and oil. Making sense and Amish thinking didn't go together."

"Hi Jake. How's your pitching arm?" Don Kemp greeted as Jake sat in the front seat.

"Guess it's okay. Haven't pitched since last spring though."

Don was in a teasing, but friendly mood as he chattered about what he expected for this coming baseball season. He teased Jake about whether he would be able to come to the practices after school this year. "You know, last year I was surprised the coach let you pitch. Why you often couldn't even come to practice," he ribbed in his friendly tone, "but then you Amish guys work so hard all the time no wonder you're in shape."

"That's certainly true. I worked enough for two people this summer. But I'll set up some hay in the barn as a backstop and practice some every day to get ready for the season. Also, this year I hope to stay for practices. After all, you play second base and you are my ride home. Besides, I have a hunch my father will okay my staying after school this year."

Jake surprised himself by being chatty with Don, but he liked him and noticed that Don genuinely liked him, and when he referred to Jake's being Amish there was no sense of being made fun of or ridiculed. Jake wondered why it felt different when the Mennonite guys on the team teased him. Their teasing seemed to carry a put down, a tone of ridicule, even meanness, as if they wanted to put distance between themselves and the Amish. He thought that maybe this was because so many English people confused the Amish with the Mennonites. He remembered in last year's history class even the author mentioned these two religious groups as if they were one and the same.

He also remembered Don was a Methodist and he couldn't tell the difference between Don and the Mennonite boys except for their pacifist stand that kept them out of the army. But in their personal lives they were not any more pacifists than anybody else. Paul Bauer, the first baseman, was one of those Mennonites who was always trying to get him into a fight. Paul was six feet tall and the school shotput record holder. Last spring during the final week of school Paul finally managed to get him into a fight. Jake had resisted all year, not because he believed in turning the other cheek, but because he could not see the point of it.

It had been raining and the team was waiting in the gym for the coach when Paul started taunting him about being a dumb Amish man. He finally gave in to his anger and frustration of the whole year and quietly said, "All year you have been trying to get me into a fight with somebody or other. Why don't you come over here and say that to my face?"

A hush fell over the team and Don had tried to intervene saying, "Cut it out, Paul. You're twice his size." Ron, another Mennonite who played right field, told Don to mind his own business and if the Amishman was dumb enough to fight Paul he deserved what he got.

Paul had swaggered onto the spot Ron was designating and trying to get the players to form a ring for the fight. Jake knew very well that some of the guys would like nothing better than to see Paul put down a notch or two. He had tried to disarm Paul by smiling and saying this obviously was no contest while keeping his wrestling stance. Paul had seemed to relax imperceptibly as he reached out his right hand. He had instantaneously grabbed the outstretched arm, spun a one-eighty and flipped Paul onto his back on the hard gym floor. He was still lying there groaning when the coach entered the silence demanding to know what had happened. Paul slowly got up and explained, "Ah, nothing, Coach. I just slipped and fell, nothing serious."

Don had been listening to the car radio, but his curiosity got the best of him. "I forgot you are not a man of many words, but I'd sure like to know what in the heck you think about sometimes."

Jake chuckled but after a pause replied, "I suppose I have to get used to how much you people like to talk, but I was just remembering the fight with Paul last year and hoping he'll leave me alone today when we get to school."

"Geez, that was something," Don said laughing. "I played in a summer league with him and he got teased a lot about how he got his ass whipped, but you won't have to worry about him, he moved out of state. But I tell you one thing, though. You sure got the respect from a lot of the other players. Besides, they like you better than some of those Mennonite guys. It's none of my business, but I couldn't help noticing you're not dressed Amish. You gonna leave them?"

"Not sure, yet," was all he could say.

After a long pause Don apologized, "I'm sorry, it's none of my business. Well, we're almost there. Look at all those cars."

Jake was glad Don changed the subject, but he wondered how Don got that way, talkative, chatty, said whatever was on his mind, and also was able to easily apologize without making a big deal of it. For the first time he was aware that this way of being so free with others seemed appealing even if it was strange. But he doubted he could ever really be that way.

"Here we are. Meet you here by the car at three-thirty, okay?"

"Sure Don, later."

Jake walked into the main building and was flustered and surprised by all the friendly hellos and joking comments referring to him as "the wrestler," as the one who scared Paul into another state, and the pitcher who was going to give them a winning season. While this open friendliness from the other boys made him feel good and wanted, deep inside he could not understand why they had to say it out loud, or why it made him so flustered and uncomfortable. He knew he did not really belong to them. But could he? Ever? At least nobody said anything about dressing like them, he thought, feeling relieved.

After English class he was trying to catch up with Don when he heard a girl calling him from behind.

"Jake, Jake, wait up."

"Hi Marcy."

"Going to the cafeteria, right?"

"Yeah, I was just trying to catch up with Don."

"How about catching up with me instead," she said with a twinkle in her brown eyes. Her dark brown hair was cut just above the shoulders and the sunlight showed a glint of reddish tinge. She wore black, a tight straight skirt, and a form fitting angora sweater.

Jake wanted to be friendly but he was at a loss. He could not decide what to do with his eyes. She was beautiful, she was sexy, but why did she have to make everything about her so obvious. Her pointed breasts demanded to be seen. He chose to merely glance at her eyes and quickly agreed to walk with her so he at least would not have to look at her then.

"You look handsome in your new clothes," she began chatting.

"Oh, they're just clothes," he lied, because he knew these clothes were many things; his rebellion, his wish to belong, his wish not to be seen as odd, weird.

"You just being modest? Or maybe you have trouble taking a compliment?"

Jake felt very confused. He did not know what to say. She was pretty. She was friendly. But she talked openly, too openly, too directly, and she could almost poke someone's eye out with her breast points. He wished just to secretly read her mind, not openly read her body.

"Gosh, you're not very friendly. I sure don't feel welcome. Doris," she called out to a girlfriend, and before Jake could try to explain that he did not mean to be rude she had already left him to join her friend.

He found Don and they ate lunch at a table with all guys and he tried to appear as if he were listening to the conversations while he was secretly trying to understand what had happened between Marcy and him. He decided he would try to learn all he could by getting Don to talk on their rides, which he knew would not be difficult to do. He needed to learn something, something about how they think, but he did not know what he was supposed to learn. He remembered the Tournier book about the psychology or meaning of personhood. Maybe that would also help him learn this "something." But what was it?

On the way home from school Jake asked Don if he knew a girl in school by the name Marcy.

"Marcy, who?"

"I didn't get her last name, but I think she is also a senior." Jake was trying to be as casual as possible, trying to convey a mere passing superficial interest, having learned at home he could always get closer to the truth by listening, not so much to the words being said, but to the tones and to the unspoken communication.

"Oh, Marcy Levin. The sexy girl in black. She was in my literature class. I'm surprised you don't know about her. Her mother's a well-known writer and Marcy has already had some of her own poetry published. She is very smart, has money, and is very particular about who she dates. Why do you ask about her?"

"Well, I, ah, just saw her in one of my classes and I thought someone called her Marcy," Jake evaded because he didn't know if Don might talk too freely about these things, and was glad he had not noticed Marcy walking with him to the cafeteria. He decided the real way to find out the truth and what he needed to learn would have to come more from what people did not say, not from what they said.

"Hey, you getting interested in her?" Don teased.

"Not possible, you already said she was particular," Jake joked back and they both laughed as he got out of the Ford and Don said he'd see him tomorrow.

During the next several months Don had no way of knowing he had become the subject of Jake's intense study as they rode back and forth to school. Jake learned that if he asked casual-toned, open-ended questions Don would respond with a wealth of information that streamed out like water from an open faucet. He was the oldest of three boys. His father was a contractor, his mother was a head nurse at the city hospital, and they lived in a new house at the edge of town on four acres of land. His main chores were mowing the lawn with a riding mower and occasionally buying the groceries for his mother when she worked the night shift. Jake repeatedly tried to imagine what that kind of life with so much leisure time would be like. But Don seemed happy, even happy-go-lucky, yet he was industrious, did well in school, and had many friends. With so much time to play and hang around, why wasn't he lazy, obnoxious, troubled, and friendless, spending his time with the rowdies who were usually in trouble with the town policeman?

Jake was not surprised that Don, a rather handsome, slim guy with black curly hair and a resonant baritone voice who he figured to be about five eleven in his bare feet, had a girlfriend. He was taken aback by how freely Don talked about his girl, Doris, Marcy's friend, where they went on dates and even what they talked about and what they did. What puzzled him the most was not his amazement about how freely Don talked about his personal experiences, but that Don was still a virgin, as were Doris and Marcy considering how sexy they dressed. This just did not make any sense. Why dress with such form-fitting clothes that revealed so much if the other message was hands off. Ellie would never be such a tease; either she did it or she didn't. She wouldn't imply by the way she dressed that she would do anything and everything, to raise the guy's excitement and then expect him to stay in the gray expanse of ignoring the obvious sexual message.

This made no sense. Jake did remember though that during the first several years at the high school he was so over stimulated that to himself he had referred to the place as the School of the Perpetual Hard

On. He no longer felt as over-stimulated as he used to, but he wondered what happened to him inside. Did something important change? Did he die a little inside? Was this what it took to become one of them?

That night as he knelt beside his bed to pray he felt a vague sense of unease, a sense of fear, of dread, of wanting to stay Amish. How could he give up his dream to learn all he could? Yet, he felt he had entered a journey, a long and strange journey, but if he did not stay Amish he had no idea where the path would lead.

He envied both his Amish and his English friends; they seemed to know where they were going. He didn't. He felt lost and utterly alone and this night his prayers, he was sure, did not reach beyond the ceiling in his bedroom. He promised God that he would do anything asked of him, even quit school and stay Amish, if God would just give him a sign of what He wanted. Peace still did not come. He tried every promise of submission to His will.

Nothing happened. He was still miserable. Finally, exhausted he climbed into bed, but he couldn't fall asleep and then he remembered the letter his mother had teasingly handed to him on his way upstairs saying it looked like a love note from his Ellie.

Chapter Eleven

Letters

The one-page letter was warm and friendly. Still, Jake sensed a heaviness, a serious tone, perhaps even an urgency even though Ellie simply wrote to say that she missed him the last three weeks and invited him to come to the Sunday Singing that was going to be held at their house a week after Thanksgiving. At the bottom of the page she had added a P.S. saying she wanted to talk to him about some new plans she had, "Lord willing."

Although he didn't feel particularly alarmed about the alluded plans because Ellie often liked to surprise him, his curiosity made him wish they had a telephone so he wouldn't have to wait so long to find out what she had in mind. Besides, he hated writing letters. He remembered Don talked to Doris almost every day on the phone. Now he envied him although he could not imagine talking to Ellie every single day even if they had one. He could not understand how Don always had so much to talk about. He himself would much rather do something with Ellie, an activity like boating, playing ball, or gardening. This seemed to be a better way of really getting to know another person. Words seemed too much like the clouds that hid the sun.

He was sure that if he listened only to Don's stream of words he would merely have a vague sense of who he was. He would have perceived Don as a friendly, outgoing, smart, and confident fellow instead of also sensing that beneath that was the Don who felt doubts about his worth, his intelligence, and even his manhood. Silence seemed to make him nervous. Jake often found himself listening to Don the same way that he had learned to sense the moods and temperaments, the trust and fear levels of the animals on the farm. This was also why he felt he knew Ellie but he would have to be with her to really know what was behind the words in her letter.

The day finally came for the Singing and his father, knowing Jake's eagerness to go, said he did not have to help with the milking that night since Sarah and her husband were still there to help. His sister and family with their four little boys, the last named after Jake, had come for the week of Thanksgiving from Ohio. Their hired driver's car had broken down and Jake was glad they were still there, especially so he could leave early to help Ellie and her family prepare for the Singing. Besides, he couldn't wait to find what surprise Ellie had cooked up for him.

He left with Nellie and the single buggy right after church services and arrived in only an hour because it was cold so he did not have to prod the pacer. Ellie was waiting for him wearing her black pea coat, a pale blue scarf that almost completely covered her blond hair, and thick black stockings that contrasted her long tan dress. Together they unhitched Nellie whose perspiration made her steam in the cold air.

"Hurry. I'm freezing," Ellie yelled over her shoulder as she ran ahead to open the stable door.

Jake took the reins and led the pacer into the barn to an empty stable that was bedded down with fresh straw. "Is this the one for me?"

Ellie had already gone to the other side of the manger to get hay and laughingly replied, "No, it's for your horse."

"Well, thanks a lot," Jake laughed as he unbridled the mare, then chased Ellie in the aisle between the double row of mangers, caught her as they fell onto the pile of hay, still laughing. He nuzzled her cheek, took her in his arms and softly asked, "Wie bist du?" But she didn't answer except to close her eyes. Her high cheek bones were red from the cold and her nose felt icy. Her lips were slightly parted. He kissed them as he held her close. Without opening her eyes she wrapped her arms around his neck and returned a passionate kiss, then just as quickly pulled away still averting his eyes.

"What is it?" he whispered. She lay quietly not answering.

"What's the matter?" he gently repeated as he sat up and took her hands in his. "It's not a surprise, is it? It is something you could not tell me in the letter, right?"

She opened her blue eyes, but only glanced at his and replied, "I'm really glad you could come today."

Jake had seen the evasiveness, or perhaps it was fear, in her eyes. He remembered her crying spell by the lake. Instead, he said, "Ellie, I also couldn't wait to see you, but don't you hide behind the nice words." His heart began beating faster. He now knew she was trying hard to hide something important. "I have to know, and you need to tell me now. What is bothering you?" he persisted.

"Checky," she added the y to his name as an endearing quality, "I'm going to go away. I have to go away."

His chest felt the sharp pain, like a stab as his heart sank, because he knew the tone, the seriousness when Ellie added that she would have to go away.

"Why, Ellie, why do you have to go? Is it me you have to leave?"

"Oh, no. I love you, Checky. That's why this is so painful."

"Then why go?" he insisted.

"Because I think it is the Lord's will."

"How can you know that? Now really!" Jake began to feel more angry than scared.

She retorted, "Come to think of it, maybe you are partly the reason. You go to school and ask so many questions that you don't even seem to believe we can know what God's will is."

"You said yourself that you wish your father let you go to high school." Jake was getting more and more frustrated and angry. He hated how she seemed to be hiding behind God's will just like Bishop John did about his brother's death. In anger he yelled, "Now why don't you just tell me the truth!"

"I did," she yelled back. "I told you I have to go away. And that I love you," she quietly added.

"But you did not tell me where you are going, and you did not tell me why you actually have to go," he persisted.

They stood there in silence for a long time. Tears began to trickle down her cheeks and Jake moved closer, took both her hands, and waited. Finally, her voice breaking, she explained, "Checky, I can only tell you that I am sure it is God's will that I leave. I'm going to Sarasota where a lot of Amish live and I already got a job in a nursing home there. I just can't tell you the whole truth right now. I have to get away from my father, but I promise I will write. Checky, I'll miss you more than you could ever know," she said as she sobbed in his arms.

"Ellie, Ellie, are you in here?" her father had stuck his head through the stable top door.

"Yes, I'm here talking to Jake," she yelled back.

In an accusing tone he chided, "Your mother needs help in the house."

"Ya, I'll be right there," she replied.

As they walked toward the house Jake resented her father, but he could not understand why she would make such a drastic move to get away from him. So maybe he was a bit harsh and strict. That did not make him any different from many of the other Amish fathers. Jake had become very fond of Ellie and now that he knew she was leaving she seemed more uniquely precious than ever. It felt like he was losing his one real confidante, kindred spirit, and soulmate from the Amish. The familiar deep ache that always started in his throat threatened to come out in tears. He kept these thoughts to himself, but changed the subject to control his emotions. Instead, he asked Ellie what kind of crowd they were expecting for the Singing.

She understood immediately, "Right, Jake, we better talk about something else. We'll put on our nice, happy Amish faces so nobody gets embarrassed about real feelings." They both laughed and she challenged him to race her to the house and just as he caught up with her, she veered to the left to circle the house giggling as she ran. When they reached the front door again she explained, "Now they can't see I was crying. Everything has to seem fine. Right?"

"I know what you mean," he whispered as they entered the porch.

. . .

Three weeks passed since the Singing and Jake still had not received a letter from Ellie. He kept reliving that afternoon in the barn and later that evening they left the others, about seventy young people from several different districts, and went for a long walk in the woods. On their way they met up with Jim Cassidy who was holding a beer bottle in one hand and a cigarette in the other apparently relating, what Jake assumed were dirty jokes, to a small group of Amish teens. Jake tried to ignore him but Jim had recognized him even though it was dark and yelled out, "Hey, wrestler, how about another match, or are you just hanging out with the girls now?"

Jake merely gave a curt nod and kept on walking with Ellie. "I can't believe that English is still trying to be Amish. Of course, he fits right in with these Amish with his drinking and smoking."

"Now Jake, you know not all Amish are that wild when they're young," Ellie chided him.

"I know," he replied, "but this Amish practice of letting the teenagers sow their wild oats until they get married really doesn't make any sense to me. How can they be so against education, which is supposed to help us become better people, when at the same time they can just look the other way when their young folks go wild. I already know of five teenagers who have gotten pregnant. They are all getting married, of course, and they'll confess their sins and join the church."

Ellie kept quiet. Jake remembered the crying girl from baptism. He continued, "When I was fifteen, the girl, Rebecca, that joined the church the same time I did, why, she was pregnant at the time. All she ever did was sit there and cry. I never did find out what happened to her. I think maybe she moved away."

"Well, maybe that was the best answer for her. Especially if the fellow wasn't Amish," Ellie replied. "But there is something to be said for the Amish boys. They take responsibility for it, right?" Ellie argued.

"Still, it all seems so hypocritical," Jake responded angrily. Ellie looked puzzled.

Jake felt more angry and added, "Did you ever notice that the preachers that are the most liked always were the wildest when they were in their teens? You know Preacher Pete Miller. Well, did you know he had even gone off to the army when he was young? Look at him now. Why, he can preach such a storm about sin and hell there is hardly a dry eye on the women's side and most of the men, of course, they can't cry so they just lean forward and stare at their shoes. Oh yeah, old holier than thou can sure preach up a storm. Especially, about the evils of sex and drinking, the very things he's probably most experienced in."

"Jake! How can you say that?"

"I just can't stand such hypocrisy. Maybe you don't know that he still sneaks his whiskey. Well I do. I saw him do it myself in their barn when we were there for supper about six months ago. I froze on the spot and made sure he didn't know I was there. Look, Ellie, I'm not for or against drinking, just against him being two-faced about it. Besides, he is always preaching about sex. It makes me wonder what he could be covering up, maybe he likes sheep,"

"Now Jake, you sound so bitter and angry. I don't like when that side of you comes out. The thing about sheep is such a crazy low blow.

You know better than that," Ellie retorted.

"But sometimes I just can't help it. I just get so mad about these things. Anyway, I know for a fact about one Amishman that messed around with calves, so just don't be too surprised if old Pete is a complete fake," Jake defended but saw that Ellie became very quiet as she stepped up her pace moving away from him. "Ellie, wait. I didn't mean to offend you. Why are you mad at me?" He caught up with her and gently took her arm. She stopped but turned her head away. "Come on, Ellie, look at me. What's the matter?" He took both hands and gently held her face. She looked up at him with tears on her cheeks glistening in the moonlight.

"I want to go back to the house," was all she could say.

"Sure, Ellie. I'm sorry I upset you. I usually don't talk so much. You know I can't say what I really feel and think to anybody. I thought it was different for us," he tried to soothe her, feeling helpless not knowing what he could say to make her feel better because he did not know why she was crying. They walked back following the wooded path with him leading the way, in silence. He felt better when she took his hand in hers as he helped her climb over the rail fence at the edge of the woods. By now they could hear the faint strains of gospel music floating on the cool night air coming from the house. She held on to his hand the rest of the way. He felt forgiven. For what, he still didn't know.

Just before they reached the house she turned to him and said, "Checky, just remember whatever happens, I love you. Also, don't forget that many of the Amish are very sincere, good people."

"I know, I know," Jake replied. "But is that what made you cry?"

There was a long pause as she looked away and in the dim light he could see that far away gaze of sadness and pain in her blue eyes. Finally, all she said was, "Once I get to Sarasota I will write you a long letter, but let's go in now and have fun, okay?"

No matter how hard he tried Jake could not shake the heavy feeling of sadness even though they were singing his favorite toe tapping English gospel songs. On the long buggy ride home he kept hearing her words that whatever happened, she loved him. But this assurance felt hollow.

Finally, a day before Christmas, a letter came post marked from Sarasota, Florida. His mother excitedly gave it to him as soon as Don drove out of the gravel driveway, for she knew very well that Jake was trying to hide his sadness about Ellie's leaving. Jake had never talked about it. Talking about feelings always seemed to obscure the real communication, so he gave up trying and relied on his sensing instead.

At the last quilting bee his mother overheard Mattie Yoder mention that Ellie had moved and taken a nice job in a nursing home. She asked Mattie to repeat the gossip and tried to find out why Ellie left, knowing the women were not aware why she was asking all those questions. She felt sad for her son and wished he would confide more in her. That night at bed time she had merely asked him if he had heard yet from Ellie. At that instant he was startled that she knew, but his face remained passive and he simply said that no he hadn't. However, she saw his pain and sadness in his eyes and he knew she knew. Nothing was said about this, but she gently put her hand on his arm as he turned to go upstairs. He slowly, quietly closed the door of his room behind him, laid down on the bed with his clothes on, and cried himself to sleep remembering Fish Lake, their walk in the woods, and the feelings of losing her and his brother Joe got all mixed together into one big soup of sadness by the time he fell asleep.

He took the letter knowing his excitement was not totally hidden underneath his matter of fact, "Danke, I'll go right up and change my clothes to do the chores." He leaned over and patted Frisky's bobbing head on his way to the house.

"You don't have to hurry, the cows can wait a little," she kindly responded.

Once he got into the house he ran up two steps at a time, closed the door, took his pocket knife from the top bureau drawer, and carefully slit the right end of the envelope.

"My Dearest Love," it began and Jake still found himself recoiling from such blunt expressions of affection no matter how much he also longed for them. The letter continued, "I am sorry I did not write sooner, but I feel so mixed up and can't seem to sort things out. I still believe it is God's will that I left my family and there was no way I could leave them without leaving you at the same time. I miss you so much! Yesterday I did such a weird thing it scared me. I took a needle and scratched your initials on my arm until it was hard to stop the bleeding. But I still hope the scars will stay. You make me feel so good as a woman, as a person, but I also know I still cannot tell you the whole truth that you begged me to write. Perhaps one day I can."

She signed it, "Love always, Ellie."

Jake read the letter four times before he hid it in the drawer with the false bottom he had secretly made when he was ten to hide his fifth-grade school photograph. At that time his mother had threatened to burn it after his sister Sarah had felt compelled to tattle on his having allowed the school to take his picture. But his worst sin that had infuriated his mother was that he willfully paid for it and brought it home. He was determined to keep it and cut a false bottom that could only be lifted out with his pocketknife. He did not want to take a chance with his mother's curiosity so he put the letter away to reread the next day, Christmas, when he would have lots of time alone.

Chapter Twelve

Christmas Day

It was a quiet cold Christmas day. Two inches of snow had fallen during the night. Jake woke up to the sounds of his father stoking the furnace in the basement and the clanging sound of the water heating up in the radiator pipes. He was glad to have a day off except for the morning and evening milking chores. When he got downstairs his mother and father were waiting for him at the kitchen table. His mother had set out a plate full of candy, an orange, and a new shirt folded neatly beside his plate. He thanked them for the Christmas treat. He especially appreciated the store-bought plain shirt because this one he could wear at school as well as at Amish gatherings.

"I'll save the candy until after breakfast," he said as he put the hard candy into a small bag. He took the bag and his shirt to his room and came down with a present for each. He gave his mother three yards of light blue cotton material for a dress and for his father a book, *The Robe*, a novel about the mystical effect Jesus' garment had on a Roman soldier.

"Oh, danke, danke. You shouldn't have, but it is so nice," his mother beamed. "This cloth has a very good weave," she added as she held the yard goods to the light from the window. Then she took her present to the dining room, set it on the table, and returned to the kitchen to prepare breakfast.

His father sat at his end of the kitchen table reading the book jacket while Jake busied himself with the plates, silverware, and water glasses. His mother stood by the counter stirring the batter for the egg pancakes. With her back toward him she quietly asked Jake, "What kind of book did you give your father?"

Jake could not see her face to read her level of concern. He tried to be reassuring by replying, "It's a good Christian book; a story about the robe Jesus wore after he came down from the cross."

His mother did not respond.

Jake added, "I think father will like it."

His father looked up from the book. "Ya," he said, "it sure does look interesting."

Jake accepted this as his thanks and knew his father's appreciation would be shown later by his comments about the story as they worked side by side. His father continued reading his book while Jake finished pouring the water into the glasses. They sat down for breakfast even before doing the morning chores, another concession they traditionally made for Christmas day.

"The eggs are ready now, just like you like them, turned over once," his mother sounded her most cheery self. "Help yourself to all the sausage you want; our last hog was so big it might last us all winter."

Jake felt relieved to hear his mother's cheery tone. If buying his father the book bothered her, her tone did not show it.

They sat down in their set places, the same places they had when Sarah and Joe were still at home. Eating breakfast before doing the morning chores felt like luxury to Jake. This was their traditional concession to honor Christmas day.

His mother picked up her bread and said, "Joe, pass the jam."

Jake and his father both looked at her. Neither said anything. Only then did she realize her slip. A depressive silence fell over the room.

Jake remembered other Christmases when Joe and Sarah were still at home and how the house was filled with noise and excitement. On Christmas morning they would wake up excited and get dressed. The custom was that Sarah, as the oldest, would be the first in line down the stairs to the table where the plates full of candy would be waiting.

He decided he would break the silence and try to get them talking about the good times they used to have when Sarah and Joe were still there.

"Remember that silly snake Joe made from an old piece of rubber? That was some present."

"Ya, and when you opened the wrapping it uncoiled and scared you half to death," his father said as they both laughed.

His mother only smiled. Jake knew that her sadness would rule her day unless he helped find something to do. So he quickly suggested, "Maybe you could start working on your new dress today; it might be fun."

She knew he knew about her depressions. She felt his kindness and replied, "That is probably a good idea. I think I will do that. It's a very nice material."

After the morning chores they all busied themselves. His mother set up her Singer sewing machine in the dining room by the big bay window. His father retired in the living room with his book and Jake went upstairs to his room to read the letter from Ellie. With the letter on his lap he sat on the bed looking out the south window. Snow covered the fields that stretched almost a half mile to the woods. The sun shining on the snow on the porch roof made him squint. In the distance he could see snow clinging to the trees at the woods edge and behind them deep, dark shadows.

He slowly opened his letter. He read and reread it over and over. He still could not understand it. The words themselves were clear enough. He felt deeply warmed by her open expression of affection for him and yet, there was something bothering, something foreboding he could not name.

He took out the stationary from his dresser determined to write a response. Nothing came. The woods kept calling. Finally, he gave up trying. He decided to take a long walk into the woods where he could be completely alone with his thoughts. Maybe the woods would help him know what to say.

"Going to the woods for a while," he said as he passed his mother cutting the pattern for her dress on the dining room table.

"It's cold. Wear your 'tsipfel.'"

"Ach, ya," Jake answered irritated. She seemed to forget his age.

He grabbed his wool cap and two pairs of gloves, pulling the gray huskers over the dark brown cloth drivers pair. By the time he put on his old black pea coat and entered the porch to step into his buckled boots, Frisky was yelping and running excitedly from one end to the next.

"Alright, alright, you can go with me," he soothed, "but we're not hunting rabbits."

The air was a crisp twenty-five degrees above zero with only a slight breeze, leaving the fresh snow tracks from the morning chores unaltered. The invigorating air was a welcome contrast from the depressive atmosphere of the house. Frisky was still darting back and forth, his white fur looking gray and dirty in the fresh white snow. When they got to the twenty-foot wooden barnyard gate Jake pulled his old trick. He climbed over the wooden fence instead of opening the gate and sprinted across the barnyard toward the half-mile lane leading to the woods. The little terrier took off full speed around the north end of the barn and caught up with him six fence posts down the lane.

Jake threw scoops of the fluffy snow into his fur and rolled him onto his back. With one quick nip Frisky pulled off Jake's right husker glove and romped toward the woods with Jake laughing in tow, unable to narrow the distance between them until Frisky teasingly let him catch up before taking off again. They played this game until they neared the fallow mint field lying by the woods when Jake lowered his voice while giving his command. He knew the message was not in the words, but in the tone. Frisky seemed to understand tones, he thought, better than people, especially those he knew at the high school.

He remembered going to the school counselor about an English project and noticing the discrepancy between the friendly words and the hostile tones. He could not determine whether or not the counselor was aware of the disparity, but he was not about to take any chances so he cut the meeting short. He vowed he would not seek help from any teachers who did not seem to know the difference between real communication and words.

They entered the woods, alert and silent. Even though they did not come to hunt, out of habit he stopped talking and Frisky held his barking, holding his short ears taut and sniffing for rabbit scents in the tiny footprints. Together they stealthily slunk on the soft fresh snow going deeper into the world of the silent woods. All was quiet and hushed except for the cawing of crows in the distance.

Even the southwest breeze did not reach them in the heart of the woods where the path turned west by the old sycamore tree; its leafless winter branches and silver-gray bark coated with sugary snow shining in the afternoon sun. Most of the snow clung to the north side of the branches revealing the direction of the storm the night before. Not an animal was in sight, but their tell-tale identities were left behind in the hunter's braille of snow tracks. A possum's walking paw prints heading east crossed over a slightly older trail of a raccoon running south. Crisscrossing these were rabbit tracks of different sizes that led to a pile of fallen branches from a dying elm where Frisky was barking furiously.

"Come, let's go," Jake called. "We're not hunting today." But Frisky did not understand until Jake walked on. He followed his favorite path that led to the eight-acre field that lay between theirs and the neighbor's woods. If he was lucky he might spot a deer crossing the opening. Frisky let go of his quest and caught up with Jake. Just as they were slinking up the last mound for a view of the open field a rabbit bounded out of hiding and the chase was on with Frisky barking as he tore through the underbrush.

"No chance for seeing deer now," Jake muttered to himself. He contented himself by watching the futile chase. Then he walked to the northwest edge of the woods where in summers he loved to sit by the creek on an old stone fence to watch the sun go down.

The water in the creek was frozen except for a hole in the ice right by the bank. Probably made by a muskrat, he thought, and remembered how he used to go hunting and trapping for muskrats with Joe. A loneliness set in like a thick fog.

Joe and he used to trudge to the creek very early in the morning to check the traps before the foxes and the raccoons stole their catch. Joe had made a short thick club that hung from a twine around his waste to finish the kill by hitting the muskrat on the head without damaging the fur. Then in the evening after supper he would help Joe skin the animal by holding the muskrat by its hind legs while Joe carefully knife-peeled the pelt. Jake remembered how he hated to do this but his wish for his brother's approval and admiration always won out.

He also remembered the one time his wish for approval did not win. That was the time Joe wanted to go hunting rabbits and he had refused.

"I don't understand. Why don't you want to go? Dad and Uncle Levi are going too," Joe had insisted.

"Because of what happened the last time."

"The last time? I don't remember anything special happening the last time we went hunting. What are you talking about?"

"It's too hard to talk about."

"Look, Jake, I won't tell Dad, or anybody. Just tell me what in the world is bothering you."

"You remember, you had the twenty-gauge shotgun, Dad had the sixteen gauge, and I had the twenty-two rifle."

"Ya, so?"

"Well, I saw this one rabbit first. I shot. I hit it. You remember? It was hurt. But it got away and I'll never forget how sick I felt when that rabbit crawled away dragging its hind leg."

"Oh, I remember that. We couldn't get it out of the brush pile. So?"

"It made me sick to my stomach. To hurt an animal like that, I'd rather kill it. Many times I even had bad dreams about that rabbit, crippled in the woods, maybe all alone, maybe it was a mother, I don't know. What I do know, I'm not going hunting again just for sport. If I have to do it because we have to eat, alright, but otherwise forget it."

Joe was quiet for a while thinking, then said, "I didn't know this; you could be teased about being a sissy, but I won't tell anybody. I know you're not a sissy. I'll just tell Dad and Uncle you have a stomachache. But maybe you'll get over this sometime," he added looking puzzled.

Jake shuddered. It was getting colder. He could tell by the sun's position that it must be about four o'clock although telling time by the sun in the winter was always more difficult, he thought. He whistled for Frisky and it wasn't until the walk back that he realized that he had not even thought about Ellie and the letter he could not write.

Chapter Thirteen

Graduation

They followed the creek north leading out of the woods. It was getting colder and Jake could no longer see the sun peeking through the treetops as it disappeared behind a thick blanket of gray clouds. From deep within the woods he could not tell how the wind had changed until they reached the edge of the woods. The southwest breeze had shifted to a stinging cold northwest wind that sucked up the snow and swirled the fine granules around his face, stinging his cheeks like microscopic pellets. Jake pulled his wool cap over his ears and down to his eyebrows as he picked up the pace down the snow-covered dirt lane fenced on both sides. The wind sweep had already layered a new white cover leaving no signs of a boy and his dog heading toward the woods. He felt cold and sad. He stopped, turned his back against the wind and looked down watching his last footprint disappear. He stood there in the cold, in the wind, in the middle of the lane. There were no boot prints showing that he had come, that he had gone, or even that he was there at all.

The lump began forming in his chest, but he did not know why he felt like crying. Then he remembered Ellie and how she kissed him that last time. He wondered if that would be the last time. "If it turned out to be the last kiss," he thought, "all that would remain would be the memory like a footprint in the snow. I will write her. No matter how difficult it is, I will tell her I love her; that I want her to move back. She would have to explain why she went away." If she didn't or couldn't, he knew it was over between them.

Frisky startled him with his yelping question, "Why are you stopping here?" He nipped at Jake's glove trying to start another game, but only succeeded in pulling him out of his reverie.

. . .

He sent his letter the first day back at school. He asked Don Kemp to stop at the post office on their way to school.

"Must be important," Don mused. "What is it, an application to a college?"

"No," Jake answered quietly as he tried to readjust from his Christmas vacation of solitude to Don's chatty demeanor. He realized Don did not mean to be nosy. He was just being friendly.

"So maybe it's a love letter, huh?" Don teased.

"I guess so," Jake replied, but was not about to give any more details and was pleased Don stopped pushing for more by changing the subject.

"I'm applying to Indiana University. My mother went there and in March or April we're going to Bloomington to visit the campus. I can hardly wait, you know, to live in a dorm, have parties, and play baseball, at least if I make the team."

"Sounds interesting," Jake tried to sound casual to hide his disappointment that he would not be able to go to college until he was twenty-one.

"Why don't you come to IU? I'm sure you could get in. If they accept me," Don laughed, "they would certainly take you with your brains. I saw the last honor roll with your name close to the top."

"I hope to, someday," Jake replied. "But I can't go until I'm of age and then I'll still have to save money before I can go."

"Of age? What do you mean?"

"Twenty-one. You see, the Amish have a custom that unless you get married you either work for your parents or you give them all the money you earn until you're of age."

"Geez! And you have to pay for it too. I'm pretty lucky, I guess. So what are you going to do for the next two years?"

"I'll work the farm and in the winter months work at a mobile home factory if I can get a job there. I think that will work out because I heard they're especially looking for cheap Amish labor. Actually, the factory was recently moved out in the country just for that purpose because they know the Amish don't believe in joining the unions."

"Well, I don't know," Don wondered, "you already broke the rule about going to high school, so why can't you break the rule about working until you are of age?"

"Because it wouldn't be fair to my brother and sister. They had to do the same thing. My dad is a stickler for fairness, and I'm sure nothing is going to change his mind about that. I even feel lucky that he let me go to high school," Jake said as the car pulled into the school parking lot. "Hey, there's Marcy."

"Where?"

"Getting out of a brand new red Chevy."

Don called out, "Marcy, what's that, a Christmas present?" as he and Jake walked over to the car.

"Yep, well it's a combination Christmas and graduation present. Isn't it a beaut?" she added while flipping her red scarf over her shoulder. She looked stunning in her black wool slacks and red and white ski jacket. "Hi Jake," she said with a friendly smile.

Jake felt his heart pounding, but he was determined not to make the same mistake with her he made before. He surprised himself as he heard his reply, "Hi. That's a beautiful car, but I can't decide which is the most gorgeous, the car or the driver."

Marcy threw her head back and laughed, moved over to Jake and put her arms around him and said that was the best line she heard in a long time and added, "It's especially nice to hear it from the man of few words."

To his amazement Jake hugged her back and kissed her lightly on her left cheek.

Don also noticed the change in Jake but only kidded, "Well, now that you two have finally met, how about taking Jake, Doris, and I on a spin to the Dogs and Suds place for lunch in your Chevy."

"Great idea. After English class? Okay, Jake?"

"Sure," was all he could say. All during history class he was trying to understand what had happened to him. Something had changed inside, he did not know what, but something that made him feel chatty like Don, something that made Marcy like him. He felt scared. He didn't know how he got there, or where this would lead him. There were no tracks to follow and the ones he had left behind were already drifted over by his emotions.

What if Marcy liked him too much? What would he do? He could never ask her for a date for that would mean having a car and dress-up clothes and all he had was his Amish suit. Besides, he didn't know what "they" did on dates. He tried to calm himself by saying she was just being friendly, that's all. Finally, he found a way out, a print from the past that he could hang on to even though it may end up being a mere memory. He had a girlfriend, that's what he would tell her. He would tell her about Ellie.

From that time on the four of them often went to lunch together either at the cafeteria or downtown to the fast food joint. Marcy had accepted his story that he had a girlfriend, but secretly he considered Ellie his Amish girlfriend and Marcy his English one even though he never asked Marcy for a date. He often felt he was still standing in the middle of the lane, neither belonging to the past nor to the future, caught in the middle of two very different worlds; one the seemingly safe, familiar but choking illogical one; the other one fast-paced, full of distractions of running from one external stimulus to another with little time for living inside, but exciting, nevertheless. Jake wished he could somehow bridge the two worlds so that he could live in the woods within that was a place of solitude full of life and yet also live in the outside world that fostered and even encouraged his individuality.

Most of the time, Jake felt this was simply impossible because he usually experienced being either in the world run by cash or the one run by rules and yet at the same time felt he did not really belong to either one. There was no one to talk to about his confusion and he certainly was not going to try the school counselor again since not even he seemed to be aware that his inner world of silence was not in tune with his outer world of words. As much as he enjoyed Marcy he wondered what she might find out about herself if she sat in the woods alone for hours. Why can't he just make up his mind, he kept chiding himself, to either stay Amish and forget college or leave them and join the English. Maybe if Ellie came back, he thought, the decision would be easier, but the letters had simply stopped coming and there was no way to reach her.

It was not until late May just before graduation when a letter from Ellie was waiting for him after coming home late from school. The senior class was required to stay late to rehearse for the graduation ceremonies and during a lull in the practice Marcy took Jake aside with an air of unusual seriousness. She blatantly told him that she had become very fond of him and that it was important that he at least meet her parents at the commencement before he disappeared forever. Tears came to her eyes. The lump in his throat stifled any words so he took her hand and she reacted by hugging him and crying on his shoulder. He felt a deep sadness, affection, and wished he would never have to let her go; yet a sense of embarrassment because they were in public view of the others. So when he came home that Friday Marcy's prints were fresh and vividly marked, totally obscuring the faded remnants of the ones Ellie had left behind in his memory. The last thing he expected was a long letter from Ellie.

Jake's curiosity felt like a wild stallion out of control, but his fear of what he would find in the letter reined him back to wait until bedtime.

During supper his mother cheerily offered more of everything, "Have more mashed potatoes, Jake. Help yourself to more homemade strawberry jam, it's the last jar. I found it in the cellar behind cans of peaches. I knew you would like it."

Jake wished he could share his mother's happy mood and he knew it was the letter from his Amish girlfriend that cheered her up. She seemed to cling to the letter like a driver hanging on for dear life to the reins of a runaway horse, not realizing the harder she pulled the faster the pacer would go. But all he could say was, "That jam is a nice surprise for May."

"I also made your special cherry pie."

"Danke schoen. What's the special occasion?"

"Oh, I just felt like it today," she said with a twinkle in her eyes as she added, "I saw the big letter that came today."

"What letter?" his father asked interrupting his meal.

"Why, Jake got a letter from his Ellie," his mother beamed.

"Oh, that," his father replied as he went back to his food having immediately lost interest. Or was he interested? Maybe he was somehow embarrassed and just pretended to lose interest. Jake wondered what his father really thought, what he felt. He felt sad realizing he would never know even if he asked.

The sun had already gone down and it was nine o' clock before Jake went up to his room. He lit the kerosene lamp beside his bed, replaced the glass top, turned the knob that raised the wick, which heightened the flame giving enough light by which to read. He sat on the edge of his bed watching the flickering flame and listening to the sad hooting owl sitting in the apricot tree thirty feet from his window before he slowly opened the envelope.

Dear Jake, greetings in Jesus's holy name [the letter began]. I'm sorry I did not write to you sooner, but so many changes have been happening to me that I don't know where to start. I met some new young Amish people here in Sarasota but they are very different from the ones you and I knew in Indiana. They like to get together and read and study the Bible. We also read it in English instead of German so we can under-stand it better.

As you can imagine the regular Amish make fun of us and think we're just trying to be more like the world. We get together every Wednesday evening. Last week one of the others threw a live mouse into the living room where we were studying. We just knelt down and prayed for them.

Being Christian is so different from being Amish and it made me realize why I had to leave you. Many times I've asked God to forgive me for what you and I did at Fish Lake. You know how our ministers often preach against sex before marriage, but everybody knows that's what they say and yet you would be laughed at if you didn't do it. These young people are different; they say it and live by it. The bigger sin, though, I've learned about was that I loved you too much. Just the other night we studied Matthew chapter twelve where Jesus said, "He that loveth father or mother more than me is not worthy of me, and he that loveth son or daughter more than me is not worthy of me. And he that taketh not his cross, and followeth after me, is not worthy of me."

So you see, I loved you too much. It scares me when I think how much, even making me scar my arm with your initials. Now I love Jesus and I pray for my father every day. I wrote him a letter encouraging him to read the Bible and tried to explain that he could stay a very good Amishman and still become a Christian and that I am trying to forgive him for what he did to me and my sister. Jake, I have never been able to tell anyone but God what happened, so please destroy this letter after you've read it, and please don't hate me for leaving you. My father had a problem with us little girls. He sometimes would play with us in the barn in a way that was very, very wrong. When we told Mother she was just as helpless as we were because he was the boss, the head of the house as he liked to say. He finally stopped bothering us when I was fourteen. I always knew I would leave home as soon as I found a way out. Maybe now you can understand that no matter how much I loved you, why I could only go so far with you and no further by the lake.

Now I am happy in the Lord. If I remember right you should be ready to graduate from high school soon. Hope you have a nice graduation. Think about becoming a Christian too, alright?

Yours in Christ,
Ellie

Jake read the letter over and over. This was not the Ellie he had known and each time he came to the end of the letter he got more and more angry. Her father had always been so righteous. Now he was not sure if he could stay Amish even if he wanted to.

Late that night when his parents were asleep he tip-toed to the basement. He crumpled up the letter and threw it into the furnace. The coals were still glowing. For a second the letter lay there, then suddenly burst into flames. He stood there with the furnace door open and watched it burn until nothing was left but small black flaky ashes.

His cheeks felt hot from standing by the open furnace and from his tears. He stood there, alone, wondering if this was his last goodbye to Ellie.

Chapter Fourteen
The Factory

The day of the commencement exercises came on a hot humid day in June. Don agreed to drive him to the school one last time although he explained he would not be able to take him back home since he and Doris and their families were celebrating afterward. Jake said that was fine although inside he was terrified, for he had no idea how he would find a ride home, but he would rather stay home than embarrass himself by driving Nellie and the buggy to the event. Finally he decided to take the chance he might find another way home and thanked Don for his offer to get him there.

Don came by at noon with his newly waxed blue Ford and looked very dapper in his light gray suit, maroon necktie over a blue shirt, and oxford tie shoes. Jake had never felt more Amish, more different from Don than on this day. He had always avoided formal occasions whenever possible for this very reason. During the regular school days he wore the store-bought clothes and was able to forget, at least momentarily, the cultural differences. But today he could not avoid his anger and envy about having to look so unlike his peers. His only hope was to wear his English school clothes and head straight to the robe room to cover up his strange garb. If he was lucky, he thought, he would already be in his gown before Marcy and her family arrived. He felt a deep shame and embarrassment even as he imagined Marcy and her parents meeting him dressed in his black Amish suit with the straight-cut high collared jacket and barn-door pants held up by suspenders.

When Jake left the house his mother was napping and his father was reading the *Martyr's Mirror*. Jake poked his head into the living room doorway and interrupted, "I might be a little late getting home from the ceremony today, but hope to make it in time to help with the chores."

His father merely looked up from his reading and nodded.

Don gave his customary friendly beep as he entered the driveway even though Jake made sure he was always respectfully punctual.

"Hi Jake. Hey, not wearing a suit for the special day?"

Jake knew Don was just being his chatty self and had no comprehension how painfully he had agonized over what to wear, and how much he had even debated about whether or not to attend the commencement. Neither could he imagine ever telling Don of his struggle or about his anger and envy. Instead, he hid his feelings behind the friendly words about how dapper and sharp Don looked. Don responded with his excitement for the celebration party that was planned.

Jake listened politely while wondering how he could hide his feelings with flattering words. Was he becoming like them, even like the school counselor? Was that what was meant by education? Would he become more false and elusive if he went on to college? He feared for himself and wished his journey had never begun for he could not know where it would lead. And yet, he could not stay with the Amish because deep in his heart he knew he had already left, never to return. He was lost in the "in between," between the rigid past and the unknown future, between the woods and the barn, between the woods within and the woods without. He could never go home again to his childhood woods of innocence. He felt utterly alone and lost. Like Ellie.

They were one of the first to arrive at the school. Jake thanked Don for the ride and excused himself saying he had to go to the john while making a beeline for the robe room where he picked up his cap and gown. Marcy arrived later wearing a white dress with a vee neckline revealing a touch of cleavage, with a matching blue belt and dark blue pumps. Her short black hair shaped her head with soft feminine curls that accented a dash of rouge on her cheeks and the touch of red lipstick.

She looked stunningly beautiful and Jake remained in his corner behind the robing seniors. He watched her unobtrusively from the other end of the long rooms. She seemed even further, worlds apart, from him than Don. The cultural abyss that separated them made Jake wish he had not come today to meet her parents, least of all to say goodbye. Goodbye to what? To someone, to something he never had or could even dream to have or be a part of? He felt the fool. Why was he even there? His shame and foolish dreams mixed with his nervous sweat and blotched his shirt beneath the robe. He sat there alone and watched the scene of friends and family congratulating their proud seniors wishing he could belong to families such as theirs. He felt alone, but glad his Amish family was not there. He preferred the sadness to embarrassment.

Whether the speaker's address was long or short he didn't know, or what was said he had no clue. He had closed his ears and eyes to the outside and in his mind he fled to the woods with his only friend. It was spring and the trees were full of leaves. The underbrush had sprung green and lush from the heavy rains that also filled the sunlit patches with wild flowers of daisies and lilies of orange and pink and violet. He and Frisky romped these pockets of aromatic and colorful spots of heaven and laughingly chased away the mating rabbits. He had just begun the search for the edible mushrooms with their brainy folds when the clapping at the end of the address reached him in the woods.

After the diplomas were finally given out one by one on the stage, he stood alone leaning against the auditorium wall feeling out of place as he watched the happy families congratulating his classmates. The whole scene seemed to be shouting for all to hear and see; HE DOES NOT BELONG! He was just about to leave to return his gown when Marcy sought him out with her mother and father behind her. He felt numb and stiff when she congratulated him with a hug.

"Jake, I want you to meet my parents. Mom and Dad, this is Jake. I've talked so much about him. I'm sure you remember."

Her father said a friendly, "Hi, Jake. I am pleased to meet you. Marcy quite admires you."

Jake could not trust the friendliness. He could only respond with a shy hello and when Marcy said she hoped to see him around, he had answered that he was sure he would. In his heart he knew this was good-bye; that he would probably never see her again.

. . .

Summer came. There was nothing to do but work. After the plowing, harrowing, and planting, came the hay season and the cultivating of the new sprouting corn. The days were long and hot. The letters from Sarasota simply stopped coming. Even his mother did not ask about them anymore. He missed her, not the Ellie that wrote the last letter, but the one he knew before she left, the teasing, laughing and tender confidante. He also missed his friends from school. He never saw them, not even Don. Their lives and paths simply did not cross. His life was on the farm, isolated from the rest of the world with no bridging radio, television, telephone, or newspaper to the outside except for an occasional buggy trip to the nearby town for sugar and flower, and their beef they stored in the rented meat locker behind the grocery store.

Jake felt lonely, sad, isolated, and cut off from the world that school had provided for him. "At least I don't have to try and live in two very different worlds at the same time," he tried to comfort himself. He even looked forward to the bi-monthly church meetings which brought a welcome relief from the isolation feeling and yet the feeling of not belonging even with them was a painful reminder of that awful experience at the graduation ceremonies. But he welcomed meeting Erv and Joseph after the services to visit or to play their game of wrestling which always reminded them of Jim Cassidy.

One Sunday in early August Jim Cassidy came to their district church services and the three of them agreed to ignore his presence. The service was held at the Lehman's home and before the nine o'clock meeting began the young men gathered in the milk house by the dairy barn. Jim walked in with his black hat cocked on the back of his head and loudly said, "Howdy boys. Well if it isn't the wrestler, Jake himself."

Erv turned to Jake and Joseph, completely disregarding the greeting and quietly said, "Meidung var bessuh, glaubet net?"

Erv couldn't keep a straight face, but Joseph dead-panned his agreement also in their dialect. They maintained their ostracism, acting as if Jim was a mere figment of the imagination, that he actually did not exist. They refused to speak English to accommodate him and purposefully did not include him in any way. Most of the other boys followed suit. Jim left immediately after the last song, stormed to the barn to retrieve his horse and angrily jerked the reins as he hitched him to the buggy with the Amish boys laughing as they watched him whipping his horse as he tore down the gravel lane.

Jake turned to Erv and said, "There is something strange about that guy, something I don't trust. Wish I knew what it was. I also feel bad we had to treat him so mean."

"Ach, don't worry about him," Erv replied. "He deserved what he got for pulling that knife at the wrestling. Besides, he is joining the other district, not ours."

"Ya, suppose you're right," Jake said although he could not agree with Erv even though he did not know why. Something did not feel right about using such a mean and powerful "meidung," the extreme ostracism they used on Jim. It would seem better to punch a guy out than what they did. He remembered how devastating it was to his mother that she was shunned by her own brothers and sisters.

"Don't be so serious, Jake. Forget about it," Erv interrupted when he saw the pensive look he had come to know. "Make sure you come to the Singing tonight. It will be held right here at the Lehman's, you know."

"Erv, I can't do that. Pop isn't feeling too good and I have to do the chores by myself tonight. Besides, tomorrow I start on my first job away from home. The trailer factory."

"Hey, you're going to make some cash. A cousin of mine works there. He told me most of the men working there are Amish and some even make as much as three bucks an hour. Your father will like that, all that money you'll make for him."

"Ya, guess so," Jake responded deciding not to tell Erv he was thinking of trying to talk his father into letting him save a portion of the paycheck for college when he was twenty-one. "Well, aufwiedersehen. See you in two weeks," Jake said as they parted.

On Monday morning Bill Fox picked him up with his station wagon to take him to the factory. Bill explained that he was his first pick-up; that he had lined up five more Amishmen to ride with him to work. "That way," he went on, "you Amishmen pay for my way to work and help pay for this new Chevy wagon."

He finished with a throaty chuckle that irritated Jake. It sounded so crass and rude making it clear that he didn't give a damn about helping provide a nice exchange, being shamelessly open about his intent to exploit the Amish needing rides in order to help himself. Bill turned toward Jake, his beer belly bouncing with the low chuckling and his cigarette hanging from his lips when he talked. Jake merely nodded his head in response.

"Now, I want twenty bucks a week and if you can't pay me right away you can give me the balance after you get your first paycheck. From then on you pay me on Mondays for the week. Got that?"

"Sure," Jake quietly replied as he gazed out the window avoiding looking Bill in the eye. In a space of a few minutes he already hated this fat-bellied cash man who did not even seem to know how insulting he was, to assume that Amishmen would have to be told to pay their bills and that they were too ignorant to know when they were being exploited. Bill reminded him of Jim Cassidy. He wondered if Bill simply did not understand, that perhaps he was new to the Amish, so he asked, "How long have you worked at the factory?"

"Twelve damn years," he spit out as if he were angry at the whole world, "ever since the company moved out of the city to get away from the union problems. They figured they could use the hard-working Amishmen who don't believe in unions. Told my boss I'd work for non-union wages if I could make it up some other goddamned way."

Jake didn't respond but decided he would find out if there was any alternative way for him to get to work. He even wondered if working at the factory was worth it if he had to ride with this crude and crass, beer-bellied cusser.

When they stopped to pick up the other rides Jake moved to the back seat giving the excuse that a taller rider should have the front seat, hoping his excuse would disguise the fact he wanted as much distance as possible from Bill. Dan Miller, a young man in his thirties from his church, took the front seat. While they recognized each other, all Jake knew was that Dan had worked for the trailer home factory for a number of years. The other riders were all strangers.

When Dan got into the car he looked around and said, "Wie gehts? Well, now, aren't you Jake, Amos's Jake? Joe's little brother, right?"

"Ya, hi Dan."

Dan continued, "Didn't know you were going to work at the factory. So what did you do, quit that high school?" he asked sarcastically.

Jake's heart sank from the stinging remark as the other Amishmen in the car turned around to look at him as if he were a poisonous snake.

To his astonishment Dan then turned to Bill and menacingly remarked, "Now that boy's gonna have to learn how to work in the real world, right?" to which they both laughed.

During the ride to work Jake was stunned as he listened to Dan and Bill talk in the manner of Bill's crude and cussing English, like two hillbillies trying to outdo each other. He wondered if that was what happened to Amishmen if they worked in the factory too long. Would they take on the characteristics of the people they worked with daily? Why wouldn't the others become more like the Amish. He had been told that over sixty percent of the employees were Amish. He did notice that when Dan came to the car he didn't wear his suspenders, but other than that he looked as Amish as he does at church with his barn-door pants, plain light blue shirt, and untrimmed beard.

Jake was deeply puzzled over Dan's inner metamorphosis and wondered if Dan was even aware of it when they arrived at the plant. He had been asked to go to the office to fill out an application. A Mr. Green, who Jake later learned would be his boss, asked him to complete the forms assuring him that he already had the job because he had come so highly recommended.

Mr. Green instructed, "Jake, when you are finished with those, I'll take you to the place in the assembly line where all the metal siding is screwed onto the mobile home. I thought I would start you with the metal gang."

Chapter Fifteen

Discovery

After completing the application forms, Mr. Green took Jake back to the station where the metal workers cut and attached the aluminum siding to the mobile homes.

"This is Paul Beachy, your foreman for the metal gang," Mr. Green introduced.

Paul merely nodded hello and looked him over while stroking his beard. When Green had left he remarked with a smile, pleased with what he surmised about Jake as a worker, "Du kannst schafe, ya?"

Jake answered, "Yes, I have learned to work very hard." Jake liked Paul immediately and knew they would make a good team. They both preferred little talk and a lot of hard work. He guessed Paul was in his early forties with a large family to feed and so had taken this job to supplement his farming income. They were about the same height and build. He knew Paul was married since he had a beard.

"Come, I'll show you a few things you have to know. We only have a few minutes. The line moves every two hours whether we're finished or not."

Jake followed Paul outdoors to the stacks of metal and aluminum sheets. They felt hot from lying in the sun. He guessed the sheets were about three and a half feet wide and ten or twelve feet long.

Paul explained very little. He merely said, "I sure was glad to get Amish help. I'm not good at explaining things. Took those hillbillies weeks to learn the job. With you, I know I can just, show. The next trailer coming through gets red aluminum. I'll pick up a sheet. You watch how I do it so you don't slice your fingers off. Ouch! It's hot. Red always gets the hottest in the sun."

Jake watched his every move. Paul leaned over the red stack, at the middle, grabbed both edges at the width, and in one quick motion bowed the middle of the sheet lengthwise to keep the sheet from buckling. Then he carried it over his left shoulder into the building to the stationary electric metal cutter.

"Now you get the next one. I'll watch."

Jake kept the image in his mind of what he had seen Paul do. He merely followed each step of the picture and as he carried the sheet to the cutter Paul said, "Cut. The others still buckle them half the time. Then we can't use them. That's when Cop gets mad."

Cop must be Mr. Green. The hillbillies must be the other two of the metal gang, Jake thought. He did not ask Paul. He knew it would be better just to learn by watching and listening. This was the way he learned how to use the power drill and the electric screwdriver that riveted the metal sheets onto the wooden studs spaced sixteen inches apart.

Paul had put him on the opposite side of the trailer from himself. No matter how hard he tried he could not keep up the pace to drill the hundreds of holes followed by drilling the screws into those holes on a sixty-foot mobile home before the line moved. Two hours had never seemed so short. It was time to watch Paul to see how he completed his side in time. After lunch he walked to the other side and to his surprise Paul did not even bother to drill the screw holes. With his powerful arms he only used the power screwdriver, holding the spinning screws with his index finger and his thumb, thereby cutting the job in half.

After several weeks Cop came by, "I want you to stop in my office during lunchtime."

"Sure," Jake had replied but he wondered if he had done something wrong.

Or maybe Ken, his slow, grumbling coworker, had complained about something. Ken was always razzing him about working too fast and hard. "Whatcha trying t'do, fix us outta da job? Dontcha know, da more ya do, da more they gonna ask? Jesus Christ, yo dumb Amishman," he'd mutter over and over.

When lunch came Jake went straight to Mr. Green's office following the long line of mobile homes in different stages of completion, past the roofing station, the side wall department, and on to the first station where they built the floors. The floor gang was already seated along the unfinished foundation eating lunch and as he was about to enter the front office he heard a familiar voice to his left.

"Well I'll be goddamned, if it isn't the wrestler."

Inside, Jake's body went on the alert, but he casually turned and looked straight into Jim Cassidy's eyes without saying a word. He merely nodded his recognition without breaking stride and went on into the office while noting Jim clearly did not even try to pass for an Amishman here at the factory. He wore a red and white striped shirt, denim jeans, and a belt.

Mr. Green looked up from his desk where he was eating his sandwich. He had a friendly look in his eyes, wiped his mouth with a napkin, and pointed Jake to a small metal folding chair.

"Well, Jake, you're doing very good work. I want to give you a raise, but I wanted to tell you in private so as not to cause any trouble. Thought two-fifty an hour would be about right," he said as he held out his hand.

"Sounds good," Jake responded as he shook his hand while his heart was pounding in his ears.

He was glad Mr. Green showed no signs of knowing how nervous he felt inside. It seemed so strange to be treated with such open and obvious respect from his superior. Paul also respected him, but with him it was something known in a felt sense. Paul would never come right out and say it and risk creating pride. Jake wondered if he could ever become comfortable with such open expressions of positive feelings from a superior.

Jake seldom saw Jim except from a distance and always avoided him whenever possible. One Wednesday it was not possible. It was late October and Cop had honored Jake by asking him to work overtime in Paul's place since Paul was not able to stay past the usual quitting time. Usually, only the department heads were asked to stay for the time-and-a-half pay hours to either finish a difficult job or repair damaged work. There had been a mistake in an order form for the fifty-foot mobile home that had come through the line that day. The order had called for turquoise aluminum siding when it was supposed to be all white. The metal gang had to correct their work and had run too far behind the assembly line pace. Working alone, Jake figured it would take him three hours to do the job.

At first, Jake thought he must be the only one working late except for Tom Johnson who agreed to give him a ride home. But Tom worked in the paint shop adjacent to the main-line building, which was eerily quiet of the din of hundreds of drills, saws, and pounding banners. All the main overhead lights had been turned off at quitting time after the hundred plus men rushed out to their rides home, leaving behind a strange silence and darkness except for two spots of light at the floor station at the front of the building and one a few stations beyond him. Only a few sun rays streaked through the occasional windows spaced far apart and ten feet above the floor requiring a ladder if you wanted to see out the window, and even those were often broken by careless workmen.

The eerie silence was broken by the sound of a lone power drill that seemed to come from two stations down the line from his. It sounded like someone reinstalling a window or a door indicated by the rhythmic pattern and frequency of the motor's grating buzz. The buzz had a high pitch when running free, a lower pitch when drilling. Then Jake recognized it as the electric screwdriver and not the driller. He stood still like a hunter and listened a while longer counting the number of low buzzes. Too many screw counts for a window, he thought, guessing it to be a door.

By six-thirty Jake finished, turned off the lights at his station, undid his carpenter's apron, and put his hammer and metal cutters into the tool box with a lock. He had learned to lock up his tools, not so much because someone would steal them, but because somebody would hide them, then gleefully watch him get behind in his work as he wasted time looking for his tools. This was one of the men's favorite antics. As he walked toward the front of the building past the line of unfinished trailers, the dying rays from the setting sun filtered through the high windows casting eerie shadows of different lengths and shades along the joists and beams close to the ceiling. Close to the floor the shadows disappeared into darkness.

He assumed all the other trusted overtimers had already punched out their timecards and gone home. The silence seemed almost deafening when he heard a crash from the front that sounded like wood splintering. His automatic instincts took over as he instantly crouched low not moving a muscle keeping his eyes locked toward the sound. Then he saw a light, a moving light, come from the office door. Must be a flashlight, he thought, which heightened his suspicions. Cop would want him to check this out, he said to himself and stealthily crept to the light. He entered the small hallway to the office. The wooden door was partially open and had been splintered beside the latch with what looked like a hatchet cut. There was a sound of ruffling papers and desk drawers being opened and closed.

Through the crack between the door and frame he could see a dim light but he could not see who was there or what they were doing. He felt trapped. His intuition told him to hide and secretly discover the intruder; his thinking said to walk on in and see what was going on. As he was trying to decide what to do the light moved again and Jim Cassidy stepped out almost bumping into him.

In that fraction of a second, Jake saw Jim's fear turn into rage, and knew, what he had only sensed before, that Jim was a dangerous animal. Instantly when he saw the fear he took his advantage and yelled, "What are you doing here, Jim?" keeping his eyes locked onto Jim's hoping to intimidate him.

It worked only for a moment until Jim's survival instincts took over. He thrust the flashlight trying to blind Jake and too late Jake saw the kick aimed at his groin. Jake went down writhing in pain, but grabbed Jim's right foot tripping him to a hard fall.

"You Goddamned son of a bitch," Jim screamed as he charged but slipped into the office instead.

Jake knew he was going for the hatchet. He took off running through the dark following the line of trailers toward the metal gang station. He pulled one of the folded aluminum ladders across the narrow path hoping to trip Jim or at least give him warning so he could open his toolbox.

Jim first followed suit, yelling and waving his flashlight, but became still and cautious once Jake disappeared into the darkness. Jake easily found the box in the dark, but had to rely on counting the clicks to open the combination lock. Jim, of course, had snapped off his light for he knew the light was only to his advantage once he knew where Jake was. Just as he opened the lock he heard Jim kick into the ladder only twenty feet away.

Jake grabbed his hammer and the power drill making sure the three-inch steel bit was securely fastened. He knew he had to get to the other side of the trailer where the long electric cord was already plugged into a socket. He crouched low to the wall wishing he could see around the corner to get Jim's location. To his left stood the stationary metal cutter table. He heard a step, held himself motionless, and hoped his breathing could not be heard.

The dark shadowing figure slunk past him holding the hatchet in his right hand looking back and forth like a stalking panther sniffing out its prey. He could have seen Jake, but he was looking too high. Jake kept his crouch two feet from the floor. Once Jim had gone the length of a mobile unit, Jake slipped out of his corner and ran around the trailer by his station to the rear side. This side had no doors and the windows were still covered with metal so the only way to get to him would be through the narrow aisle from either end.

Jim had heard the movement and came running back flashing his light. He caught sight of Jake going to the back side and jumped through the door into the mobile home not knowing the windows of the rear wall were still covered with uncut metal. This gave Jake just enough time to plug his drill into the long forty-foot cord. Now he was ready, with his hammer and his drill. He situated himself in the middle of the aisle at the ready for Jim charging in from either end. He waited.

Jim came from the front holding his flashlight with the left and the hatchet with his right. "You bastard, I got—"

Jake pulled the trigger of the power drill, the sound crashing through the stillness. Jim stopped in his tracks.

For the first time Jim realized his predicament. He was even more enraged. He couldn't kill Jake now, but if he didn't, then what?

"Where the heck are you, Jake," Tom called from the front door.

"Back here, Tom," Jake yelled as loud as he could. "You better come and help."

"Where are you?" Tom heard the alarm in his voice and came running back feeling his way along.

"Back by the metal department." Jake yelled hoping Tom would get the alarm.

By the time Tom got there Jim had taken off toward the back of the building.

On the way home Jake's shirt was still drenched with perspiration and he found himself unloading the whole story from the beginning since the first time of the wrestling match in the barn and all the events of the evening. Tom agreed they would report the incident of the office break-in to Mr. Green in the morning. Also, to Jake's delight, Tom further agreed to give Jake a regular ride to and from work from now on. They set a fee for this but Jake kept the reason for his delight secret. He could hardly wait to tell Bill Fox he would have to find another sucker.

The next morning before the starting buzzer he and Tom reported the break-in. Mr. Green took it nonchalantly saying, "Yeah, this happens every once in a while. He got away with about fifty bucks."

That afternoon Cop stopped by the metal station. "Listen, Jake. You've got to come to my office right away. The police want to talk to you."

Jake dropped his tools and hurriedly caught up with Cop. "He was some kind of killer, wasn't he?"

"You better believe it. You could have been killed here last night. Jim Cassidy is not his real name," Cop added, his face showing a fear and anger Jake had never seen before.

They stepped into the crowded office. It was clear that the husky uniformed officer half sitting on the desk was in charge. "I'm Lieutenant Brodsky," he introduced himself, his tone showing he had little time or patience. "What's your story, young man? We already know his real name. Hell, we almost had him at one time about a year ago after he escaped from prison. The sonnabitch killer just disappeared into thin air."

Jake told him the same story he had related to Tom the night before about his suspicions; this strange fellow wanting to join the Amish church; about pulling a knife during a wrestling match; that in no sense did he seem to want to really learn the Amish way or language.

When he was finished all the lieutenant said was, "I'll be damned. Well, I'll just be goddamned. He was smarter than any of us had imagined.

Joining the Amish to hide from the law. Now that's a pretty darn good disguise. Besides, who would ever think of looking for a hardened criminal among the gentle people." He seemed to be talking more to himself than to anyone in particular and Jake sensed the officer's voice carried a certain fear, or maybe it was admiration for the criminal. He found this very puzzling when—

"Thanks for your help, Jake." They shook hands and on his way out Brodsky turned back toward Jake and asked, "You sure you wanna build houses?"

Cop laughed as he answered instead, "Hey, you leave him alone. He's my man."

Chapter Sixteen
Woods Within

Jim Cassidy didn't show up for work again, but it was about a month before Jake got enough nerve to ask Cop if he ever found out what happened to him. He was looking for the right moment to approach his boss for he was afraid to seem too buddy buddy in front of the other employees. At all costs he wanted to avoid being considered a brown-noser. Cop had walked back to the line to give Paul a change in an order sheet for the next mobile home. Jake moved over to catch the information and then quietly asked him if the police or the FBI had caught the criminal.

Mr. Green had replied with surprise, "It was in the paper a couple of weeks ago. You didn't see it?"

"I'm sorry, we don't get the paper," Jake answered a bit embarrassed. He wished he would not have asked. He felt ashamed and stupid. He overheard a little gossip from some of the English workers during coffee breaks, but he never paid too much attention to gossip. He had learned that the gossipers usually revealed much more about themselves than about the people they were supposedly talking about.

"Oh, that's right. Forgot you Amish don't get the news," Cop replied without a hint of an accusatory tone. "Someone in LaGrange got suspicious. He was hanging around a shoe shop. It was closing time and the guy called the police who recognized him from an FBI photo. He wasn't wearing his Amish clothes anymore."

"What was his crime before?"

"The paper said he had held up a liquor store and killed the owner with a knife. It was brutal, sick. They took him back to the Michigan City Prison."

The buzzer sounded. Jake went back to work and decided there was no point in telling Cop about the knife. He felt validated, though, with the information about the killer. "I'll have to remember," he told himself, "to pay close attention when I get that sense of something wrong. My animal sensing works not just on animals." He also remembered how it had worked on Don too. He had become fond of Don, though, and wondered how he was enjoying the university.

That evening after the milking was finished Jake told his father what he had learned about the knifing killer. Fortunately, his father was in a conversational mood and he wanted to ask him the hardest thing he had ever directly asked. But, instead, they talked about Jim.

"I could never understand why someone from the outside would even want to join the Amish. It just doesn't make sense," Jake puzzled.

"The only other time I ever heard of such a thing was in Holmes County," his father began. "There was a small Amish church there. They were so strict they didn't even let anybody marry outside that little group. And you know they thought the worst thing that could happen was for a girl to be an old maid. Well, this one girl was going to get married no matter what it took, but there were no boys left her age. She got herself in a bad way with one of the English boys from the village. He was lazy, probably hadn't done a whole day's work in his life. Well, she convinced him to join the Amish. It took several years and two babies before the church finally let him join. He learned to dress Amish. Let his hair and beard grow. Part of the problem was he was too dumb to learn the language. Anyway, to this day he is tolerated, not really accepted."

Now I know why Jim Cassidy tried to join, but didn't he just make a fool of the Amish? I heard he talked to the ministers in the North District. Don't you think they should have caught on? Surely, he was a phony. The first time I met him I sensed something about him that smelled rotten, but I couldn't know for sure what it was."

His father creased his brow taking his time to think about the questions and Jake was getting impatient waiting, but had learned to give him time to think. Together, in silence, they walked to the hog pen to tend to the pigs. Jake went on to the corn crib, bucketed the right number of ears, and then went to the house for the leftover vegetable peelings his mother kept in the slop pail.

When Jake returned to slop the hogs his father was bedding the pen with fresh straw and just as Jake had given up his father responded, "In the end, Cassidy made a fool of himself. We can all be fooled sometimes."

His father continued, "I bought a horse once. At a sale barn he obeyed commands. I petted him, talked to him. Good looking too, well fed, but sleek strong muscles. A roan. His mean, stubborn streak didn't come out until I had him for a week. He sure had me fooled. Had to sell him. Figured he could never really be broken in. Lost money on him, too. Couldn't sell as a driver; wouldn't have been right."

"But somebody sold him to you as a driver," Jake interrupted. "Was the seller Amish?"

After a long pause his father replied, "Ya." His father was thinking again then finally said with a chuckle, "Well, he just cooked his own goose. How many Amish buyers are going to line up to buy his horses and livestock from now on?" and they both laughed.

Jake chose this moment to ask the question that was burning on his mind the whole evening. "I want to ask something that is very hard for me to ask. But I've been thinking about it for a long time. It's about college."

His father's expression did not change. He only waited for Jake to go on while leaning his elbows on the wooden railing that separated them from the slurping noisy hogs.

"This sounds strange, but I don't think I really have a choice. I have to go to college. If not next year, then the year after I'm of age. So, do you think it would be possible for us to arrange a way for me to go next fall? I'll almost be twenty-one."

"But how would you pay for it?"

Jake was so surprised and delighted by this question for it meant that the answer was not a categorical no. His ready response had been thought out many times. "I make eighty dollars a week at the factory. The boss likes my work so any raises I get, I thought, maybe that amount could be saved to help and the rest I would have to borrow. Also, the counselor at the high school told me I won a scholarship that would help pay for the first year. Just hope it's still there for next year."

His father replied almost immediately and it was obvious he had thought about Jake and college.

"I've always tried to be fair; to treat everyone in the family the same." His eyes showed a far-away look. He was remembering Joe.

"Joe, I'm sure, would have gone too," he mused. "Sarah is settled nice with her own life and family," he added talking out loud more to himself than to Jake as he stayed leaning on the railing.

Then he turned to Jake and said, "You make more money than I expected. So you give me every other check. The others you save for yourself."

Tears started to well up and Jake wanted to hug his father knowing that would never do. He could not remember the last time they hugged. Such an open show of affection was just not done.

But it was too late; the moment passed. His father picked up the slop bucket and what sounded like an afterthought added in a rather stern tone, "You will have to let mother know about your plans."

"I know," Jake quietly replied.

· · ·

By the third week of the following August all the college plans were in place and Jake was bursting with excitement. His seasons seemed confused. Fall was coming, but it felt like spring after a long hard winter. The budding hopes and dreams of the long cold fallow season were pushing from deep inside; pushing for the nourishing sun and water to feed the germs of inquisitive curiosity.

And yet, at times, bouts of sadness gushed over him like a dam that gave way to the reservoir of years of silent feelings. Fall was coming. A time for dying, of goodbyes. A time of falling leaves clinging to their familiar home, clutching to their brief life of two seasons. The spring buds had sprouted and grown, become old, familiar, and safe, swaddled in downy quilts of illusionary tradition.

"But that is not our way," his mother had repeatedly protested when Jake had explained his plan to go to college.

It was June. Tom had dropped him off from the factory. He and Frisky were going through their usual greeting ritual when his mother had stormed out through the porch demanding to know what kind of mail he was getting. She thrust a large manila envelope into his face.

He took the mail and saw the return address. "It's from a place in Virginia. I'll look at it after supper and see what it's about," he said, knowing how she would react. Now he could no longer avoid the talk he had been dreading for a long time.

"You still have that idea in your head, don't you," she yelled.

Jake looked at her hoping this would not throw her into one of those week-long depressions, not aware that his eyebrows raised slightly.

She misread his look and got even more angry. "Don't act like you don't know what idea I'm talking about. That letter is from a college. I can read, you know."

Now he was angry and despite his better judgement yelled back, "I know you like to snoop in my mail. And yes, I am going to college. Just like Joe would have done, too."

As he stormed off to his room to change into his milking clothes, he glimpsed her ashen face that only a moment before had been red with anger. He felt only angry, at first, but then the badness feelings stole into him like a pervasive fog. He felt badly that he yelled at her for he knew the guilt price he always paid watching her crying softly to herself in her rocker by the window. But he still seethed inside the heavy fog of badness feelings.

Once again he was faced with two terrible choices. If he was true to himself he would have to leave the Amish and go to college, which threatened to destroy his mother. But if he pleased her it would be tantamount to selling his soul to the devil of illusion. So if he was true to himself, he was bad to her. If he was good to her, he was bad to himself. He again decided he did not really have a choice. He would just have to hope that in time she could adapt.

That evening she angrily served supper, but refused to eat with them, staying in the downstairs bedroom. Jake did the dishes and joined his father in the living room where he was pouring over some farm bills. After a few minutes Jake left for his own room upstairs because he could not tolerate hearing his mother's sobbing from the next room.

For the next several weeks Jake avoided her as much as possible. Her depressive state filled the atmosphere like an invisible toxic gas accented by an occasional escaped sob, or muffled cry, a clutched handkerchief, and for good measure, periodically, a prayer said loudly enough that was meant to be overheard. She was determined. She did not mean to manipulate, only to show her love and fear for his soul. Frequently she made unconscious slips of calling him by his dead brother's name and Jake would try to assure her by saying he was just going away to college, not dying, although he also knew that he was dying to a way of life that raised in her the awful spectacle of everlasting punishment of burning in hell.

She had already lost one son in death. Now she was losing Jake to the world. Maybe this one was harder. She was determined.

But so was Jake. He knew he had the edge because she loved him; that she especially could not see surviving the loss of another son; that she would never play the ultimate card of shunning.

Bit by bit she relinquished her sincere, yet unconscious manipulative power-plays, meant to induce the conformity of a good Amishman and by August she had returned to her giving ways that said more than a thousand words. She made all his favorite pies, polished his shoes, and once when he overslept gently awakened him rather than yelling accusatively.

That evening she even asked him to help her with the supper dishes and Jake was delighted, not because he liked doing dishes, but because it was an invitation to sing. As a family, when Joe and Sarah were still home, they often passed the time singing while doing the dishes. His mother taught them how to harmonize by ear, and singing old German folk songs always lifted her spirits. His father would often join them in the large country kitchen and sit by the table, after the plain yellow oil cloth had been wiped, and listen, occasionally suggesting another song.

That night after "O, Du Lieber Augustine" and "Gott Ist Die Liebe" she started a sad song in English that had been one of their favorites. She began the gentle soft melody. He caught the mood and added a quiet harmony. They were standing by the sink, looking at the dying sun through the west windows. She washed. He dried. Her hands slowed down to the tempo of the song as they sang:

Twilight is stealing over the sea,
Shadows are falling dark on the lee,
Gone with the night wind
Voices of Yore
Seeking that far off shore.

[After this verse his father sat dawn by the table smiling and joined in the refrain.]

Far away beyond the starlit skies
Where the love-light never, never dies,
Gleameth a mansion filled with delight,
Sweet happy home so bright.

At the beginning of the second verse Jake motioned his father to join them standing by the counter. To his surprise his father stood between them, and encircled them with his arms as they sang. His mother stopped washing. Jake clutched his towel. Together they watched the deep reds on the western horizon, their voices barely singing above a whisper. His mother's tears dripped into her dishwater. The lump in his throat threatened to crack Jake's voice. They never finished the song; it fused into the stillness as they stood there, together, watching the dying light fade into twilight, held in his father's strong arms.

Jake wished they could stay like that forever. He could not re-member ever being hugged by his father although he was sure it must have happened when he was very young. He desperately wanted to hug him back, but instead excused himself, kissed his mother goodnight, closed the door of his room and wept.

The next day would be his last Sunday at home before leaving for college. It was the in between church Sunday and more than anything else he wanted to go to the woods one last time. He was glad there were no services because he hated saying goodbye to friends. He had pur-posely told Erv sometime ago that he was leaving to avoid last minute emotional goodbyes. Erv had intuitively understood and rarely brought up the subject except in a teasing, lighthearted way. Jake was sure that Erv also understood that their lives were going to go very different paths, and that even their friendship would probably never be the same again.

Right after Sunday dinner he and Frisky left for the woods. The midday sun was hot and only a few fluffy clouds drifted lazily in the clear blue sky. Frisky romped back and forth in the fenced-in lane with his tongue hanging out trying to get Jake to chase him.

"It's too hot for that," Jake kept trying to explain, wishing there would be some way to tell Frisky that he was going away and that he would miss him. He tried to hug him, but the Terrier just didn't understand as he squirmed out of his arms and wanted to play.

Halfway to the woods they were already secluded, hidden between cornfields on both sides of the dry dusty lane where the young leafy green corn had already reached a height of six feet. The stalks proudly wore their young tassels like new hats and the corn ears were beginning to bulge underneath the husks. In another six weeks, he thought, the green would have turned to brown, the corn would be ready for husking, and for the first year ever he would not be here to help with the work. He felt sad.

They crossed the dirt bridge over the shallow creek and leisurely wound their way along the thick shady overgrown path leading back to the sycamore tree. Frisky playfully chased the scampering rabbits and squirrels barking as he went, making Jake wish he could feel playful instead of solemn and sad. He remembered how excited Don had been about leaving home and going off to the university. But Don was just going to school. He was not leaving his home, his culture, his way of life, his solitude, and leaving a grieving mother at home.

He walked on, veering away from the path, avoiding the nettles and thorn bushes cropped in bunches around the section of maple trees to the south. The maple leaves were showing a tinge of color around their edges announcing the coming of fall. He continued on to the lone birch with its smooth gray bark still carrying Ellie's initials he had carved with his pocket knife several years before. The initials had enlarged with the growth of the tree. Tears welled up as he stood there remembering.

"Goodbye, Ellie," he whispered. "Goodbye, birch. Your mushrooms were always the biggest and best."

He realized Frisky had not followed him and he was alone. He stood still for a long time leaning his back against the tree. The breeze came from the northeast taking his scent away from the heart of the woods. An hour passed, perhaps two, as he stood motionless, all senses alert and open to the rich life within the woods. Crows cawed from the treetops behind him while a woodpecker attacked the oak to his right like a miniature upside-down pump handle. Jake wondered how he could keep the battering going on and on without getting a headache. Rabbits emerged from the underbrush slowly hopping from one small clump of clover to another. He imagined the wind carried a few stray seeds of clover from the hay field that took root there as he watched the bunnies hold their pink wiggling noses in the air with their ears erectly taut.

Only fifteen feet away a mother possum with its long ratty furless tail slowly ambled by carrying three young ones on its back, ignoring the bushy-tailed squirrels playing tag in her path. Suddenly the rabbits seemed alarmed and ran off. Jake waited, wondering what frightened them when a light orange fox with his nose a mere inch off the ground trotted past the fallen elm. That's when he saw Frisky stalking from the left, his belly scraping the trodden reedy grass. He was ready for attack with his ears pointing straight back, his eye-teeth bared, and his legs bunched beneath him like v-shaped buggy springs.

When Frisky sprang from his crouch Jake yelled, "Go get 'em, boy," and sprinted behind Frisky watching the futile chase as the fox quickly outdistanced him. They last saw the fox disappear over the five-foot rail fence that separated them from the neighbor's woods.

On the way home Jake stopped by the creek bridge, turned one last time toward the woods and said goodbye. He hoped he would now be able to hold the woods within to keep him close to his own true self no matter what strange and different worlds and cultures he might explore. He bade goodbye to the road his father traveled and began his journey without a clue where it would lead.

Stopping by Woods on a Snowy Evening

By Robert Frost

Whose woods these are I think I know
His house is in the village though;
He will not see me stopping here
To watch his woods fill up with snow.

My little horse must think it queer
To stop without a farmhouse near
Between the woods and frozen lake
The darkest evening of the year.

He gives his harness bells a shake
To ask if there is some mistake.
The only other sounds the sweep
Of easy wind and downy flake.

The woods are lovely, dark and deep,
But I have promises to keep,
And miles to go before I sleep,
And miles to go before I sleep.

Call of the Woods

In Spring of year I heard your call,
Come here, my son, within my shade
And listen to the breezes play
Their yearning songs of burning love.
But I was only ten.

When Summer came I heard your call,
Your branches swaying to the strains
Of songs your leaves sang in the rain.
But sadness filled my heart instead.
My brother Joe was dead.

When Autumn came, I barely heard
Your rustling leaves call from the woods,
For I had learned the "English" way
Of using words to hide my pain.
My Ellie went away.

Then Winter came with howling winds
And bitter cold and snows so deep,
I could not hear your gentle call
At all, from deep within the woods.
And I was all alone.

Alone I stayed in solitude.
The silence burst, and then I heard,
From deep inside, the singing birds
And rapping hares, raccoon, and deer
Within the scented woods.

In silence now I hear the call,
Not from a far and distant woods.
The call I hear comes from inside
The woods within, the woods within
My soul, my searching soul.